THE PREGNANCY AFFAIR

BY
ANNE MATHER

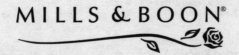

MILLS & BOON®

First published in Great Britain 2007
Harlequin Mills & Boon Limited,
Eton House, 18-24 Paradise Road, Richmond, Surrey TW9 1SR

© Anne Mather 2007

ISBN-13: 978 0 263 85319 3
ISBN-10:   0 263 85319 5

Set in Times Roman 10½ on 12¾ pt
01-0507-47854

Printed and bound in Spain
by Litografia Rosés, S.A., Barcelona

THE PREGNANCY AFFAIR

CHAPTER ONE

THE sign informing passengers to *Fasten Seat Belts* flashed on above Olivia's head and she automatically reached to check that her belt was in place.

'We'll be landing at Newcastle International Airport in fifteen minutes,' the saccharine-sweet voice of the flight attendant announced smoothly. 'Please ensure that all your hand luggage is put away in the overhead lockers and that your tray tables are securely stowed.'

The aircraft dipped to begin its approach to the airport and Olivia's stomach lurched in protest. But it wasn't the amount of coffee she'd consumed that morning that was giving her such a sickly feeling. It was the knowledge that she was returning to Bridgeford after so many years that was tying her stomach in knots.

The landing was swift and uneventful. The airport was busy and the plane taxied efficiently to its unloading bay as passengers and crew alike began gathering their belongings together. There was little chit-chat. This was primarily a business flight, most of the passengers either on or returning from business trips, with only a handful of holiday-makers to make up the numbers.

Olivia's trip was neither business nor pleasure, she thought, and she wasn't at all sure she was doing the right thing by coming here. She doubted her father would want to see her, whatever reassurances her sister had given her, and there'd be no sympathetic shoulder for someone who'd messed up her life, not just once, but twice.

Still, it was too late to have second thoughts now. The plane had come to a complete standstill, the door was open, and her fellow passengers were all jostling to be first to alight. Eventually, of course, she had to get up and follow them. She should have worn flats, she thought as her ridiculously high heels caught in the metal of the stairway. But pride was a stubborn companion and Olivia was determined not to appear as desperate as she felt.

A short walk across the tarmac and she was in the terminal buildings, offering her passport for inspection and lining up to collect her suitcase from the carousel. She'd only brought one suitcase, leaving the rest of her belongings in storage in London. Because that was where she was going to find herself an apartment, she told herself firmly. This trip to Bridgeford was just to prove to herself—and her family—that she wasn't afraid to come back.

Her suitcase was one of the first to appear and Olivia pulled a wry face as she hauled it off the carousel. OK, she thought, it was time to face the music. Linda, her sister, had said she would come to meet her. Which was a relief. She was likely to be the least-judgemental of the family.

Beyond the doors, a crowd of people was waiting to greet the passengers, many of them carrying name boards to identify themselves. One thing, Olivia thought drily, there was no way she wouldn't recognise Linda. Whether Linda would recognise her was another thing altogether.

And then she stopped dead in her tracks, the suitcase she was towing behind her running on into the backs of her legs. But she hardly noticed the bump or the momentary discomfort it gave her. She was staring at the man who was standing at the back of the crowd of people, and, although she couldn't believe it, it seemed he was waiting for her.

She glanced quickly behind her, half convinced he wasn't looking at her at all but at some other person who'd followed her through the doors. But there was no one immediately behind her, no one else to coincide with his line of vision.

And then, to confirm her disbelief, he moved towards her, pushing his way through the waiting mob to fetch up by her side. 'Hi,' he said, taking the handle of the suitcase from her unresisting hand. 'D'you have a good journey?'

Olivia stared at him blankly. 'What are you doing here?' she asked, aware that it probably wasn't the politest thing to say in the circumstances, but she couldn't help it. If she'd been anxious on the plane, she was a hundred times more nervous now. Her heart was pounding, the blood rushing through her veins like wildfire. What the hell was Joel Armstrong doing here? She'd have expected him to avoid her like the plague. 'Wh-where's Linda?'

If he noticed the stammer, he gave no sign of it. 'At home,' he replied evenly, and because he started walking away from her, she was obliged to follow him. 'Your father's having a bad day,' he continued. 'She thought it would be wiser not to leave him alone.'

Olivia blinked. She could have said all her father ever had were bad days in her estimation, but she didn't. She was too busy trying to keep up with his long strides. Trying to ally herself, too, to the man who was walking beside her. Fifteen years ago, he'd been little more than a boy. Now he was a man.

And what a man, she thought, permitting herself a covert look in his direction. He'd always been tall, but now he'd filled out, the shoulders of the leather jacket he was wearing owing nothing to padding she was sure. A lean jawline showed just the trace of a five o'clock shadow, while his unruly dark hair was shorter than she remembered, exposing the handsome shape of his skull.

Not that handsome described him exactly. His youthful good looks had given way to a harsher profile altogether. Fans of lighter skin flared from the corners of his cool grey eyes, while deeper ridges framed the narrow-lipped beauty of his mouth.

God, he was attractive, Olivia thought, feeling a pang of awareness she'd never expected to feel again. It hardly seemed possible that they'd once been married. Had she really allowed a sense of pride to rule her reason? Would things have been different if she'd chosen to stay and fight?

She stumbled as they stepped out into the watery sunshine of an April day. It had been cool in London, but it was amazingly mild here. As Joel turned at her muffled exclamation, she regretted the urge she'd had to dress up for the journey. She'd wanted Linda to envy her her trim figure and designer clothes. She'd even chosen the shortest skirt in her wardrobe to show off the slender length of her legs. As for how much it had cost to have the ash-blonde highlights in her honey-brown hair renewed... She must have been crazy to think anyone would care.

'You OK?' Joel asked now and she nodded automatically.

'I'm fine,' she said quickly. 'Where are you parked?'

'Not far away,' he responded, slowing his pace a little. 'Be grateful it's not raining. It was earlier.'

Olivia pulled a face, but she refused to answer him. Dammit, here they were, meeting one another after fifteen years, and all he could talk about was the weather. Why was she feeling so tongue-tied suddenly, when he was obviously quite at ease with her?

Whatever had happened to him in the last fifteen years had definitely changed him. And for the better, she mused. He'd left school at eighteen and, despite getting excellent results, he'd gone to work for her father. He'd wanted to marry her and they'd done so as soon as she was eighteen. Everyone had expected it would last, even Joel. Or at least she'd thought that was what he'd believed. Looking at him now, she was beginning to wonder if that was just another of her many mistakes.

'So—how are you?' she managed at last, relieved when they turned between the aisles of parked cars. Surely it wouldn't be much further. 'It's been a long time.'

'Hasn't it just?' he agreed, a faintly mocking twist to his mouth as he looked at her and Olivia knew damn well he'd never looked at her like that before. It was as if she amused him. 'You seem OK,' he added. 'I guess living in the States agrees with you.'

It didn't, actually, Olivia was tempted to respond, but that had had more to do with the man she'd been living with than with the country itself.

Joel stopped behind a huge four-wheel-drive and juggled his keys out of his pocket. Flipping open the rear door, he stowed Olivia's suitcase in the back and then went round and opened the passenger door.

Olivia was still admiring the vehicle, its mud-splattered wing in no way detracting from its sleek appearance. Was this Joel's or her father's? she wondered uncertainly. Whoever it was, things at the farm must definitely be looking up.

'Nice car,' she said, and wished he wasn't watching her get in. The seat was high and her skirt rode up to her bottom as she levered herself onto it. And she was fairly sure Joel was suppressing another of those mocking smiles.

'I like it,' he said, without expression. He walked around the bonnet and climbed in beside her, the high seat offering no obstacle to his long legs. 'All set?'

'As I'll ever be,' said Olivia tartly, not seeing why he should have it all his own way. Then, as his hands gripped the wheel, she noticed the wedding ring on his third finger. Not the ring she'd given him, she realised, but a much more expensive band altogether. Her stomach tightened unpleasantly. 'Are you married?'

It was an impertinent question and she knew as soon as she'd voiced it that it was nothing to do with her. But dammit, he had been her husband first. Didn't she have a right to know if he'd replaced her?

'Do you care?' he countered now and, despite her determination not to let him see how she was feeling, Olivia felt the hot colour stain her cheeks.

'I—not particularly,' she muttered, turning her attention to a plane that was just coming in to land. 'This airport's busier than I remember.'

'Things change,' said Joel, reversing out of the space

and turning in the direction of the exit. 'And I'm divorced. For the second time,' he appended drily. 'I guess neither of us has had any luck in that direction.'

'What do you mean?'

Olivia's eyes were drawn to him now, and he gave her a sardonic look. 'Linda told me your second marriage broke up,' he said. 'Isn't that why you're back in England?'

Olivia expelled a resentful breath. Linda, she thought irritably. She might have known her sister wouldn't keep something like that to herself. 'I've come back to England because my work's here,' she retorted shortly. 'I don't know enough about the US housing market to get a comparable job in New York.'

'Ah.' Joel allowed the distinction, but Olivia still felt as if he didn't believe her. 'So you're going to do what? Join an agency in Newcastle?'

'London, probably,' she responded swiftly, hating the need she felt to justify herself in his eyes. Why did she care what he thought of her? If Linda hadn't seen fit to ask him to meet her, they might never have had this conversation.

Joel used the ticket he'd bought earlier to let them out of the car park, and then turned north towards Ponteland and Belsay. The sky had cleared and it was that shade of blue that seemed almost transparent. The trees were already greening with spring growth and here and there late daffodils bloomed along the hedgerows. Olivia had forgotten how beautiful the countryside could be. Living first in London and then New York, she'd become so much a city animal.

'Um—how is my father?' she asked at last, realising she was to blame for the uneasy silence that lay between them.

She tried to adopt a humorous tone. 'Still as irascible as ever, I suppose.'

'He has good days and bad days, as I'm sure Linda's told you,' answered Joel, permitting her a rueful grin. 'But since the stroke—'

'The stroke?' Olivia didn't let him finish. 'What stroke? Linda said nothing about a stroke.'

Joel blew out a breath. 'Didn't she?' His tone was flat. 'Well, maybe I shouldn't have either. I dare say the old man doesn't want it broadcasting to all and sundry.'

'Hey, I'm not "all and sundry"!' exclaimed Olivia, her efforts at conciliation forgotten at his words. 'I'm his daughter. Don't you think I have a right to know?'

Joel's thick dark brows arched indifferently. 'I suppose that depends on the kind of relationship you two have had over the years,' he remarked mildly. 'How long is it since you've seen him?'

Olivia huffed. 'You know exactly how long it is. I wasn't exactly encouraged to come back after—after we split up.'

Joel regarded her for a brief compelling moment. 'Is that supposed to be an excuse?'

'No.' Olivia felt herself colouring again. 'It's the reason why I haven't seen him. I have phoned, and written letters. I've never had a reply.'

Joel moved his shoulders in a rueful gesture. 'I didn't know that.'

'No?' Olivia wasn't sure whether she believed him. 'Well, why would you? I dare say you hoped you'd never set eyes on me again.'

Joel shook his head. 'You're wrong, Liv. I got over what you did years ago. I moved on. I got married. I had a son.

I realised we were too young when we got married. Neither of us knew what we really wanted out of life.'

Olivia had to force herself not to turn and stare at him now. He had a son! Of all the things he might have said, she realised that was the least expected. And the most painful, she acknowledged as the bile caused by too many cups of black coffee rose sickly in the back of her throat.

She had to say something, she thought, aware that she was taking too long to make a rejoinder. And, dammit, why should she care if he had a child? It wasn't as if she was the maternal type. But, all the same, it hurt. It hurt deep inside her. Like a wound that had been partially healed that was suddenly as raw and painful as the day she'd lost their son.

'Well—good,' she said at last, hoping he couldn't hear the thickness of her voice. 'But, even so, I wish Linda had warned me.'

'I imagine she was afraid that if you knew the truth you might change your mind about coming,' observed Joel shrewdly. 'Ben Foley isn't the best of patients. Without Dempsey's help, the farm would have gone down the drain long ago.'

Olivia was surprised. 'Martin?' she said curiously, speaking of her sister's husband. 'Does he work at the farm as well as at the garden centre?'

'They let the garden centre go,' replied Joel, accelerating past a tractor. 'They live at the farm now. It seemed the most sensible solution in the circumstances.'

Olivia was totally confused. When she'd gone away, Joel had virtually been running the farm for her father, and it had been understood that he'd take over when Ben Foley retired. That was one of the reasons why her father had been so angry with her when their marriage broke up. He'd depended on Joel. A lot. She caught her breath suddenly. Surely he hadn't punished Joel because she'd walked out?

They turned a bend in the road and suddenly it was possible to glimpse the sea in the distance. Redes Bay gleamed in the early-afternoon sun, shimmering like a mirage in the desert. Bridgeford was just a mile from the sea as the crow flies. A little further than that on the twisting roads that honeycombed the area.

'You must be hungry,' Joel said, glancing her way again, and Olivia managed a faint smile. But the truth was she felt too knotted up inside to care about an empty stomach. Though there was no doubt she'd probably feel better if the amount of coffee she'd consumed wasn't sloshing about inside her.

'I expect Linda will have a meal ready for you,' he continued. 'She still makes the best steak and kidney pie in the neighbourhood.'

'Does she?' Olivia felt even queasier at the thought of all those calories. In recent years she'd become accustomed to eating sparingly, always watching her weight for any fluctuation, living on tuna fish and what her sister would call rabbit-food. The idea of sitting down to a lunch of steak and kidney pie horrified her. Even empty, as she was, she knew she'd never get it down.

'It looks as if you could use a few extra pounds,' remarked Joel, slowing at yet another crossroads, and Olivia wondered at his perception. It was as if he'd known exactly what she was thinking.

'Oh, does it?' she said, her incredulity giving way to resentment. 'I suppose you prefer women with more flesh on their bones.'

Joel chuckled. He actually chuckled, and Olivia was furious. 'You could say that,' he agreed, and she badly wanted to slap him. She knew she was looking good—by New York standards, at least—and it was mortifying to have him *laugh* at her.

'And I suppose your second wife was everything I'm not,' she flung at him angrily, uncaring at that moment how peevish she sounded. 'Well, where I come from women care about their appearance. We don't all want to be milch cows!'

Joel sobered. 'No, I think you proved that when you got rid of our baby,' he retorted harshly, and she realised that for the first time she'd caught him on the raw. His jaw clamped shut for a few moments, as if suppressing another outburst, but when he spoke again he had himself in control. 'Forget it. I shouldn't have said anything.'

Olivia swallowed, remembering she'd promised herself she wouldn't say anything if she saw Joel either. But she couldn't stop herself. 'For the record,' she said unsteadily, 'I didn't *get rid* of our baby. At the risk of repeating myself, I had a miscarriage. Believe it or not, these things happen!'

Joel's tanned fingers tightened on the wheel and she saw his knuckles whiten at the pressure he was putting on them. 'Whatever,' he said flatly, but she knew he didn't believe her now any more than he'd believed her before. 'We'll be there in a few minutes. I'll drop you off and then I've got to get back to college.'

Olivia blinked. 'To college?' she echoed blankly.

'In Newcastle,' he agreed, without elaborating.

'You're at college?' she persisted, staring at him incredulously.

'I work at the university,' he corrected her drily. 'I gather Linda didn't tell you that either.'

Olivia's jaw dropped. 'No.'

In actual fact, Linda hadn't mentioned Joel at all. That was why she'd been so surprised to see him at the airport. She'd assumed she'd have to meet him sooner or later at the farm and that Linda was being tactful by putting off the evil day.

'Have I shocked you?'

Joel had relaxed again and Olivia knew she had to say something or run the risk of appearing envious. She'd never gone to university, although she had eventually taken an economics degree at evening classes.

Not that she'd ever needed it. By the time she'd graduated, she'd already been working in a large London estate agency. Her aptitude for the job, and the fact that she got on so well with the clients, had accelerated her climb up the corporate ladder. At age twenty-six, she'd already been earning a high five-figure salary, with added perks like her one-bedroom apartment in Bloomsbury.

Of course, she reflected, she'd given it all up when Bruce Garvey asked her to marry him. Despite her success at work, her life had seemed empty, and she'd found she missed her friends and family and the life she'd had in Bridgeford. She'd even missed Joel, though she'd been sure she'd never forgive him for walking out on her.

'I expect your parents were pleased when you left the farm,' she said at last, hoping she didn't sound as bitter as she felt. She moistened her lips. 'I'm sorry. I assumed you were still working there.'

Joel shook his head. 'I couldn't stay after—well, after what happened.'

Olivia's eyes went wide. 'You mean, my father asked you to leave?'

'Hell, no.' Joel gave her a satirical look. 'Not everything revolves around you, you know. I did what I should have done years ago. I took my qualifications and got myself a degree in IT at Leeds University.'

Olivia blinked. 'IT?'

'Information technology,' he said patiently. 'Computers, for want of a better word.'

Olivia pressed her shoulders back into the soft leather of the seat. 'I see.' She paused. 'I'm glad things have worked out so well for you.'

'Oh, yeah.' Joel was sardonic now. 'Two failed marriages and a child that might or might not have been aborted. Life's been peachy, Liv. So how has it been for you?'

CHAPTER TWO

FORTUNATELY, Olivia was saved the need of answering him. They'd reached Bridgeford and the Lexus splashed through the ford at the edge of the village before accelerating up the slope to the village green. She could pretend she hadn't heard him, pretend she hadn't been knocked off balance by the callousness of his words. Struggling with emotions she didn't even want to acknowledge, she looked instead at the Georgian homes and the handful of cottages that circled the village green. As a shiver of remembered agony slid down her spine, the beauty of her surroundings was a blessed panacea.

The village, at least, didn't seem to have changed much, she thought gratefully, although she could see the roofs of some new houses just visible beyond the trees in the churchyard. There were daffodils blooming here, too, and the almond blossom was just beginning to appear.

'Do your parents still live in the village?' she asked a little stiffly, feeling obliged to say something. The Armstrongs had never approved of Joel's relationship with her, and even after they were married Olivia had been left in no doubt that Mrs Armstrong didn't consider her good enough for her son.

'My father's retired now,' replied Joel amiably enough. Mr Armstrong was an accountant and had used to work for a firm in Chevingham, a small town some ten miles south of Bridgeford. 'They still own the house in Blades Lane,' he added, 'but they've recently bought a place in Spain. They spend a lot of time there in the winter months. They're in El Fuente at present, actually.'

Which explained a lot, thought Olivia cynically. She wondered if Joel would have been so willing to come and meet her if he'd had to explain himself to his parents first.

They passed the house Joel's parents owned on their way to the farm. Rose Cottage was set a few yards back from the road, screened by a tangle of wild roses that blossomed profusely in the season.

It reminded Olivia irresistibly of when she and Joel were teenagers. How many times had she come running down from the farm to find him waiting for her at his gate? They'd both attended the comprehensive school in Chevingham and the school bus used to pick them up at the end of Blades Lane.

Of course, Joel had been a year older, and once they'd got to school there'd been no opportunity to be together. Was that why their relationship had progressed so swiftly? she wondered. Had the excitement of forbidden fruit coloured that youthful infatuation?

'Does everything look the same?' Joel asked abruptly, and Olivia was grateful for the reprieve. She'd been in danger of remembering things that were best forgotten. As Joel said, they'd both moved on.

'Pretty much,' she said after a moment, forcing herself to take an interest in her surroundings. They were turning between white-painted gateposts now, crossing a cattle-grid that caused the vehicle's wheels to vibrate, and then accelerating up the drive to the farmhouse itself.

When the Lexus stopped, Olivia knew the journey was over. However, she felt—and she really wasn't feeling very good—she had to get out of the car and face whatever was to come. It would have been nice, she thought, if her father had invited her here. But it was Linda who'd suggested this visit. Linda, who'd told her so little of what to expect.

'You OK?'

She realised that Joel was looking at her now, probably wondering why she hadn't opened her door. And, dammit, she so didn't want to show him how she was feeling. Joel, with his new career and his precious son.

So, 'Why wouldn't I be?' she answered, with assumed lightness. She gathered her handbag into her arms and reached for the door handle. 'Thanks for the ride, Joel. It's been—illuminating.'

Now, why had she said that? she chided herself impatiently, as Joel's eyes narrowed on her face. 'Why do I get the feeling that you're mad at me?' he countered, but before Olivia could say anything else, Linda came out of the house.

At once, Olivia fumbled with the door catch, as eager to get away from Joel as she was to greet her sister. But she was all thumbs and, without asking her permission, Joel leant past her and thrust the door open for her, the hard strength of his forearm pressing briefly against her breasts.

She scrambled out then, dropping down from the high seat, almost ricking her ankle in her haste to get away from him. Steadying herself against the wing, she mentally squared her shoulders before starting a little uncertainly across the forecourt.

'Hi, Linda,' she said, in what she hoped was a confident tone. 'It's good to see you.'

Her sister shook her head and Olivia was surprised to see tears in her eyes. 'Oh, Livvy, it's good to see you, too,' she exclaimed eagerly and, opening her arms, she gathered the other girl into a welcoming hug.

Olivia was shocked. She hadn't expected such a warm greeting. Linda had never been a touchy-feely kind of person and when they were younger any contact between them had always been initiated by Olivia herself.

But evidently the years had mellowed her, and when she drew back she regarded Olivia with what appeared to be genuine affection. 'I'm so pleased you decided to come,' she said. 'This is still your home, you know.'

Olivia was trying to absorb this when Linda's eyes moved beyond her to where Joel was standing beside the Lexus. 'Thanks, Joel,' she added. 'We owe you, big time.' She paused. 'You'll come in and see Dad, won't you?'

'Not right now,' said Joel, opening the back of the car and hauling out Olivia's suitcase. 'I've got a tutorial at four o'clock, I'm afraid.'

A tutorial!

So he was a lecturer, no less. If Olivia was surprised, Linda clearly wasn't, going to take charge of Olivia's luggage without further argument. 'Well, come back soon,' she said, as he climbed back into the vehicle. 'Just because Livvy's here, you don't have to be a stranger.'

'Yeah, right.'

If Joel's response was less enthusiastic, Linda didn't

seem to notice it, and, with an inclination of his head towards Olivia, he reversed the car across the yard. Still cringing from the childish name her sister had always called her, Olivia was motionless, and it wasn't until he'd driven away that she realised she hadn't even waved goodbye.

Pulling herself together, she went to rescue her suitcase from her sister. 'I can take that,' she said, but Linda wouldn't let it go.

'In those heels?' she asked, with just a trace of the animosity that had blighted Olivia's childhood after their mother died. 'No, I can manage. Come along. I've warned Dad to expect you.'

'You didn't warn me that he'd had a stroke,' ventured Olivia as she climbed the shallow steps after her, and Linda's back stiffened in what might have been resentment.

'I thought it was wiser,' she said as they entered the square hall of the farmhouse. She set the suitcase down at the foot of the stairs and then went on, 'You know how sensitive he's always been about his health. And if he'd thought you were only coming here because he was ill…'

'I suppose.' Olivia shrugged, half understanding her reasoning. 'So how is he? Joel said very little.'

'Oh, he's improving every day,' Linda assured her. 'But you'll soon see for yourself.' She paused. 'You, on the other hand, look half-starved. I suppose you're on one of those fancy diets.'

Olivia caught her breath. 'I'm fine,' she said, wishing she dared say that obviously Linda didn't worry about her weight.

'Oh, well, you know best, I dare say,' remarked Linda carelessly. 'Come on. We'll go and see Dad before I show you your room. His bed's in the old morning room. It saves him having to climb the stairs. I hope you don't mind, but I've given you Mum's old sewing room. Jayne and Andrew have our old rooms and Martin and I are sleeping in the main bedroom at present.'

Olivia nodded. She didn't much care where she slept. She had the feeling she wouldn't be staying very long. But she had forgotten about her niece and nephew, who'd been little more than babies when she'd left Bridgeford. Jayne must be eighteen now, with Andrew a year younger. Jayne was the same age as she'd been when she'd married Joel, she reflected incredulously.

'So are the children in school?' she asked as Linda led the way across the hall, and her sister turned to give her an old-fashioned look.

'You've got to be kidding!' she exclaimed. 'Jayne works at a dress shop in Chevingham. She's doing really well, actually. And Andy's probably gone into Alnwick with his father. Martin said he needed to pick up a new rotor arm for the tractor.'

Olivia couldn't hide her surprise. 'I see.'

'I suppose you think we should have encouraged them to continue their education as you did,' went on Linda, a note of aggression in her voice now. 'Well, it didn't do you much good, did it? For all Dad scraped and saved to let you stay on at school, you just upped and married Joel Armstrong as soon as you were eighteen.'

Olivia was taken aback. She hadn't known her father had had to scrape and save to let her stay on to take her A levels.

All the same...

'In any case, we don't have a lot of money to throw around, Livvy,' Linda continued. 'What with losing the cattle to foot-and-mouth, it's been a struggle, I can tell you. We got some compensation from the government, but it's never enough. That's why Martin's trying to persuade Dad to diversify—'

She broke off abruptly at that point and Olivia couldn't decide whether Linda thought she'd said too much or because they were nearing her father's door and she didn't want him to hear what she was saying. Whatever, she lifted a finger to her lips before she turned the handle, putting her head around the door before advancing cheerfully into the room.

'Dad,' Olivia heard her say in a sing-song voice as she followed her in. 'You're awake. That's good.' She glanced behind her. 'Livvy's here.'

Her father made some kind of gruff response, but Olivia could barely hear it. However, when she managed to circle her sister's bulk to see the man who was lying in an armchair by the windows, a rug covering his bony knees, she thought she could understand why. The stroke had evidently left one side of Ben Foley's face paralysed and his hair was completely grey. When he spoke he did so with apparent difficulty.

'Hi, Dad,' she said, very conscious of Linda's eyes watching her. She struggled to hide the shock she felt as she went closer and bent down to kiss his lined cheek. Then she forced a smile. 'It's been a long time.'

Ben Foley grunted. 'Whose fault is that?' he got out thickly, and she was relieved that she could understand him.

'Mine, I guess,' she said, although she doubted he would have welcomed her back any sooner. When she'd lost the baby her father, like Joel, hadn't believed her explanation. And, when he'd heard she and Joel were splitting up, he'd told her to find somewhere else to live.

She wondered now if he'd have felt the same if he'd known Joel was going to leave the farm. They'd been sharing the house with her father and, although it wasn't the best arrangement, it had been all they could afford at that time. Joel had already moved out of the house, but she guessed her father had hoped he'd come back after her departure. Perhaps he had, but not for long. It must have been a bitter pill for Ben Foley to swallow.

Trying to put the past behind her, she went on, 'Well, I'm here now, Dad. So how are you feeling?'

'How do I look?' demanded her father, with a little of his old irascibility, and Linda bustled forward to lay a conciliatory hand on his shoulder.

'Livvy's only showing concern for your welfare,' she said soothingly, but Olivia couldn't help wishing she'd leave them alone. 'Now, do you want some tea? I'll make us all a cup while Livvy settles in.'

Ben Foley scowled. 'I thought she'd come to see me,' he muttered, giving his younger daughter a look from beneath a drooping eyelid.

'I have,' began Olivia, but once again Linda intervened.

'You'll have plenty of time to talk to Livvy later,' she said firmly, tucking the rug more securely about him. 'Come along,' she added to her sister. 'I'll show you where you're going to sleep.'

Joel slept badly and was up before seven the next morning, making himself a pot of coffee in the sleek modern kitchen of his house.

The house was large, but graceful, situated in a village just half a dozen miles from Bridgeford, where his ex-wife still lived. He'd bought it, ironically enough, after he and Louise had broken up. With four bedrooms and three bathrooms, it was really too big for his needs, but it meant Sean could come and stay whenever he liked.

He came fairly often, for weekends and holidays. Joel and Louise had had a fairly amicable divorce, both admitting they'd made a mistake in rushing into marriage. Louise had married again, and, although Joel wasn't overly fond of her new partner, he had been forced to concede that Sean should make his permanent home with them.

Still wearing nothing but the cotton boxers he'd slept in, Joel moved to the kitchen window, staring out over the large garden that happily he employed a gardener to keep in order. An expanse of lawn, where he and Sean played football, stretched away to a hedge of conifers, and beyond the hedge there were fields where sheep and their newborn lambs grazed.

It was all very peaceful, but Joel felt anything but untroubled at the present time. The smooth tenor of his life had been disturbed, and no matter how often he told himself that Olivia's return meant nothing to him, he couldn't quite make himself believe it.

Seeing her again had definitely unsettled him. When he'd agreed to go and meet her, he'd anticipated coming away with a certain smug satisfaction that he'd done the right thing all those years ago. What he'd expected, he realised, was that the image he'd kept of her all this time would have been flawed by age and experience. But it wasn't true. Instead, she was just as lovely, just as sexy, as he remembered.

Which annoyed the hell out of him. Dammit, just

because she'd taken care of her appearance didn't change the woman she was inside. The most beautiful creatures in the world could be deadly. Even so...

He scowled, rubbing his free hand over his jaw that was already rough with stubble. Then, swallowing a mouthful of his coffee, he turned away from the window and started towards the door. He needed a shave and a shower, not necessarily in that order. He'd probably feel better if he could look at himself without immediately noticing the bags beneath his eyes.

He'd made it as far as the stairs when the doorbell rang. He glanced at his wrist, realised he wasn't wearing his watch, and cursed under his breath. What the hell time was it? Not later than seven-thirty, surely. It had to be the mail, but he wasn't expecting any parcels as far as he knew.

He set his cup down on the second stair and trudged back to the door. The wooden floor was cold beneath his bare feet and he wished he'd stopped to put on a robe. But who knew he was going to have to face a visitor? he thought irritably. Particularly this morning, when he was feeling so bloody grumpy to begin with.

The door was solid oak so he couldn't see who it was until he'd released the deadlock and swung it open. Then his eyes widened and he stared disbelievingly at the child who was standing outside.

'Sean!' he exclaimed blankly. But then, noticing that the boy was shivering, Joel hurriedly stepped back and invited him in. He closed the door as Sean moved inside, dropping a backpack he'd been carrying on the floor. His brows drew together. 'How the hell did you get here?'

Sean shrugged. He was tall for his age, lean and wiry,

with Joel's dark hair and colouring and his mother's blue eyes. He was approaching his eleventh birthday, and in recent months Joel had noticed he'd developed an increasingly stubborn attitude.

'I caught the bus,' he said at last, moving into the kitchen. 'Got any cola?'

Joel paused in the doorway, watching as his son took a can of cola out of the fridge and flipped the tab. 'There are no buses this early in the day,' he said, as Sean swallowed thirstily. 'Does your mother know you're here?'

'She will soon,' said Sean, removing the can from his lips and glancing about him. 'Can I have something to eat?'

Joel sucked in a breath. 'What does that mean, exactly? *She will soon*.' He repeated what his son had said. 'Come on, you might as well tell me.'

Sean shrugged. 'I've left home,' he said, opening the fridge door again and pulling out a pack of bacon. 'Can I make myself a sandwich? I'm really hungry.'

Joel stared at him. 'Hold it,' he said. 'Before we go any further, I want you to explain how you got here and why your mother doesn't know yet. Then I'll ring her and put her mind at rest.'

'I shouldn't bother.'

Sean was fiddling with the plastic wrapper of the bacon but before he could go any further his father stepped forward and snatched it out of his hands. 'Answers, Sean,' he said. 'Then we can talk about breakfast. Why are you shivering? For God's sake, have you been out all night?'

'No.' Sean was indignant, but Joel didn't believe him.

'So where have you been?' he demanded.

'I can walk, you know.' Sean hunched his shoulders. And

then, seeing his father's expression, 'All right, I spent the night in the barn up the road.' He grimaced as Joel showed his horror. 'It wasn't so bad. There was some straw in the loft and a horse blanket. It smelled a bit, but it wasn't bad.'

Joel stared at him. 'So how come your mother doesn't know yet?'

'How'd you think? She and the hulk went out last night and they don't usually check on me when they come in.'

'Don't call Stewart "the hulk",' said Joel, though he had to admit Louise's second husband did have a beer belly. 'And what are you saying? That they went out and left you in the house on your own?'

'Hey, I'm old enough,' protested Sean, eyeing the bacon enviously. 'Look, couldn't we just have something to eat before you phone Mum?'

Joel hesitated, then he tossed the bacon back to him. 'I'll ring your mother,' he said resignedly. 'Don't set the place on fire.'

'Thanks, Dad.' Sean grinned now. 'D'you want some, too?'

His father shook his head. 'I'm going to take a shower after I've made that call. If you're cold, just adjust the thermostat on the Aga. You know how, don't you?'

Receiving his son's assurance that he did indeed know how to adjust the stove which heated the entire house, Joel went across the hall to the stairs again and rescued his coffee. As expected, it was cool now, but he intended to ring Louise before doing anything else. And from his bedroom. He had no intention of allowing Sean to listen in.

His ex-wife answered the phone with a note of irritation in her voice. 'Yes?' she said, and Joel guessed she'd probably had a late night. For the first time, he resented the fact that she and Stewart had custody of Sean. What kind of role models was he being faced with every day?

'It's me,' he said abruptly. 'Do you know where Sean is?'

'Still in bed, I expect.' Louise didn't sound worried. 'I've banged on his door and told him he won't have time for any breakfast, but does he listen? No way. Anyway, if you want to speak to him, Joel, you'll have to wait until tonight.'

The temptation to say 'OK' and ring off was appealing, but the last thing Joel needed was for Stewart Barlow to accuse him of kidnapping his son. 'He's not in bed, he's here,' he said, without preamble. 'As you'd know, Louise, if you'd bothered to check on him last night.'

Louise was briefly silenced. She wasn't used to Joel criticising her and he guessed she was wondering how to respond. 'Are you saying he's been with you since yesterday evening?' she demanded, after a moment. 'Don't you think you should have taken the trouble to let me know before this?'

'How do you know I didn't ring last night?' asked Joel flatly.

Another silence. Then, 'So he has been with you all night? Oh, Joel—'

'No.' Joel interrupted her. 'I was only making the point that you weren't there, even if I had phoned.' He sighed. 'I thought children had to be at least thirteen before being left alone.'

Louise sighed. 'We weren't out for long—'

'Even so…'

'What's he been telling you?' She sounded suspicious now. 'He can be a little monkey, you know.'

'I know.' Joel was reluctant, but he had to be honest. 'As a matter of fact, he only arrived on my doorstep a few minutes ago.'

'So where did he spend the night?' She sounded worried now.

'He says in a neighbour's barn.'

'My God!' Louise was horrified. Then she hesitated. 'So why didn't he come to you last night?'

'I'm afraid I was out, too,' said Joel unwillingly. 'I had a meeting at the college. I didn't get back until late.'

'So you weren't part of the welcome-home committee for Olivia Foley?' teased Louise, not without a touch of jealousy. 'I expect you've heard she's come back to see her father.'

Joel quelled his impatience. He had no desire to discuss Olivia's return with his ex-wife. 'If I'd known Sean was likely to turn up, I'd have been here,' he retorted shortly. 'And I don't think you should have left him alone in the house.'

'I don't, usually.' Louise was defensive. 'But Stewart wanted to go out and I didn't think there was any harm in it. We were only down the road, for goodness' sake! If he'd needed anything, he had the pub's number.'

'Whatever.' Joel wasn't prepared to discuss it over the phone. 'Look, I haven't had time to talk to him yet. I need to find out why he decided to do a bunk. Give me the rest of the day, can you? I'll give you a ring tonight.'

'But what about school?'

'He can take a day off, can't he? It wouldn't be the first time, I'm sure.'

'What do you mean?'

'Nothing.' Joel backed off. 'Come on, Louise. Give the kid a break.'

Louise was obviously not happy about the situation, but she decided not to be awkward. Perhaps she was afraid Joel might report her to the authorities. The custody order could be changed in his favour if he chose to complain.

'Well, OK,' she said at last. 'But I think you should bring him home tonight.'

'We'll see.'

Joel didn't argue, but he didn't promise anything either. He still had to find out why Sean had chosen to run away.

Fortunately, he only had one tutorial this morning and he could take his son to the university with him. Sean could play on the computer in his office while he was in the lecture hall.

His coffee was cold now, and, putting it aside, he studied his reflection in the mirror above the bathroom basin. He didn't look good, he thought ruefully. He looked as if it were him, and not Louise, who'd had a heavy night.

He wondered now why he'd married her in the first place. It wasn't on the rebound. Well, not precisely, anyway. After Olivia left, he'd wasted no time before applying for a place at university, and the next four years had passed with the minimum amount of pain.

It wasn't until he'd returned to Bridgeford that the whole sorry mess of his marriage to Olivia had come back to haunt him. Had he thought that marrying someone else and having a child would make him happy? It hadn't, although the son they'd had meant everything to him. And he was determined to ensure that Sean didn't suffer because of his mistakes.

CHAPTER THREE

OLIVIA was in her room, sorting through the clothes she'd brought with her and wondering whether a trip to the nearest town for reinforcements was needed, when Jayne knocked at the door.

Since her arrival a few days ago, her niece had become a frequent visitor, always making some excuse for disturbing her, finding reasons to stop and chat. Olivia guessed the girl found the fact that her aunt had lived in New York for several years fascinating, and her obvious admiration was reassuring in the face of her brother-in-law's hostility.

Not that Olivia had seen that much of Martin Dempsey, thank goodness! Apart from the evening meal, which they all shared, he spent much of his time outdoors.

'Hi,' Jayne said now, coming into the room at her aunt's summons and casting an envious eye over the clothes spread out on the bed. The girl was tall and slim, much like Olivia herself, but her hair was russet-coloured, like her father's, and her features were almost completely his. 'Oh, my, what are you doing?' She fingered the ruched sleeve of an ivory tulle shirt. 'You have such beautiful clothes.'

'Thanks. I think.' Olivia pulled a wry face. 'I was just

wondering if I ought to buy myself some jeans and a couple of T-shirts. I didn't bring a lot of clothes with me and those I have brought don't seem appropriate somehow.'

'Who says?'

Jayne spoke indignantly, but Olivia could tell she wasn't really interested. And Olivia knew better than to say the girl's father resented her being here. Martin apparently didn't like women who showed any independence, and her clothes seemed to be an added source of aggravation.

Jayne perched herself on the end of the bed and regarded her aunt consideringly. 'Can I ask you something?'

'You can ask.' Olivia was half amused.

'Well, were you really married to Joel Armstrong?' she ventured, and Olivia was taken aback.

'Yes,' she said at last, warily. 'Why do you want to know?'

'Oh…' Jayne looked a little embarrassed now. 'I just wondered. I mean, Mum said you were and I believed her. But since I've got to know you, you don't seem the type to—well, play around.'

'Play around?' Olivia caught her breath. Was that what they'd told her?

'Yeah, you know. There was another man, wasn't there? Or so Mum says.'

'There was no other man.' Olivia spoke tersely. 'We were just—not compatible. It didn't work out. That's all.'

'Really?' Jayne stared at her. 'Cos, like, he's really hot, don't you think? Or no, I suppose you don't. But he drives that really powerful SUV, and I think he's, like, totally the man!'

Olivia was stunned. Did Linda know her daughter thought of Joel in this way? Obviously she didn't share her confidences, and the last thing Olivia needed was one of his groupies on her own doorstep.

'I think I ought to finish sorting these things,' she said at length, not wanting to offend the girl, but not wanting to continue this conversation either. For heaven's sake, Joel was old enough to be Jayne's father.

'Oh—yes.' The girl got up from the bed now and pressed her fingers to her mouth. 'I've just remembered. Grandad wants to see you.' She pulled a face. 'He said to say he'd like you to come down.'

Olivia didn't know whether to be glad of the invitation or sorry. She'd been looking forward to finishing this task and then taking a bath. She'd discovered it wasn't wise to expect to have the bathroom to herself in the mornings. Someone was always hammering on the door, asking how long she was going to be.

'OK,' she said now, and, seeing Jayne admiring a silk camisole, she picked it up and tossed it across the bed. Perhaps it would take her mind off other things, she thought hopefully. 'It's yours,' she told her when Jayne looked up at her with disbelieving eyes. 'If you'd like it.'

'Would I?' Jayne was evidently delighted, cradling the scrap of lace to her chest. 'Thanks so much, Aunt Livvy,' she added gratefully. 'I've never worn anything as sexy as this.'

Olivia managed a faint smile at her pleasure, and, passing the girl, she opened the door and allowed her to precede her from the room. But she hoped it wouldn't prove another black mark against her. With a bit of luck, Martin Dempsey might never find out.

Downstairs, she bypassed the dining room, where Linda and Martin were still sitting. She could hear their voices, though not what they were saying, and instead she made her way along the hall to her father's room. She'd visited him several times in the last few days, but this was the first time she'd been on her own. Usually, either Linda or Jayne was with her, ostensibly to ensure that the old man didn't upset her.

Tonight, however, Jayne had scurried off to her room. Probably to try on the new camisole. Which meant Olivia entered her father's room without an escort, feeling almost conspiratorial in consequence.

He wasn't in his chair tonight, he was in the bed across the room, and, closing the door behind her, Olivia crossed the floor. 'Hello,' she said, when she saw his eyes were open. 'How are you tonight?'

'Better for seeing you,' he muttered, and, although his words were slurred, they were perfectly audible. 'I see you managed to shake off your watchdog.' He lifted his good arm and gestured for her to take the chair nearest to him. 'Come and sit down where I can see you.'

Olivia didn't know if he was joking about her having a watchdog, but she acknowledged that Linda and Martin did want to know where she was every minute of the day. 'Thanks,' she said, deciding not to take him up on it. 'I must admit, I've wondered how you felt about me coming back.'

Her father frowned. 'Because of what happened with young Armstrong?' he demanded.

'Well, yes.'

He nodded. 'That was all a long time ago.'

'You never answered any of my letters,' she reminded him painfully. 'According to Linda, you rarely mentioned my name.'

'Yes, well, we all make mistakes, Liv. Mine was in not seeing you were too headstrong to take any advice from me.'

Olivia sighed. 'If it's any consolation, I haven't exactly made a success of my life.'

'No?' Her father's lids twitched in surprise. 'I heard you were doing well in London. Of course, then you upped and went off to America with that man, Garvey. I gather that marriage wasn't happy either.'

Olivia bent her head. For a moment she'd been tempted to say that her marriage to Joel Armstrong *had* been happy. Until she'd discovered she was pregnant, that was, and panic had set in.

She could remember well how she'd felt at that time. It wasn't how she'd have felt now, but that was irrelevant. Then, all she could think was that they were both too young to have a baby, that they couldn't afford another mouth to feed. She'd wanted Joel's baby, of course she had. She'd spent hours—*days*—trying to find a way out of their dilemma that wouldn't entail her losing the child. Like any other would-be mother, she'd fantasised about what it would look like, whether it would take after him. But the problems had seemed insurmountable at first. After all, they could barely support themselves.

But her father wouldn't want to hear that. He and Joel had been on the same side and she had no intention of trying to change his mind now. So instead, she said, 'I should never have married Bruce. I made the mistake of thinking that because he said he loved me, I'd have everything I'd ever wanted.'

'Was he wealthy?'

Olivia shrugged. 'I suppose so.'

'Was that really why you married him?'

'No.' Olivia shook her head. 'Believe it or not, I was lonely. I needed someone who'd care about me. He was smart and good-looking and it seemed like a good idea at the time.'

'You were lonely?' Her father picked up on that. 'So why didn't you come home?'

'I didn't think I'd be welcome,' she confessed honestly. 'And—well, I assumed Joel would still be here.'

'He left. A couple of weeks after you went to London.'

'Yes, I know that now. But not then.'

'Linda kept in touch with you, didn't she?'

'Yes.' But her reports were decidedly selective, Olivia thought, though she didn't say so. 'Anyway, it's all in the past, as you say.'

'So tell me about this man you married. Bruce Garvey. What went wrong? Did he treat you badly?'

'No.' Olivia sighed. 'It's a long story, Dad.'

Her father made an impatient gesture. 'Well, I'm not going anywhere, as you can see.'

'Why not?' Olivia used his words to try and change the subject. 'Don't you have a wheelchair? Don't you ever go outside?'

'I don't want a wheelchair,' retorted the old man grumpily. 'Bloody things. They're for invalids. I'm not an invalid. I'm just—stuck here, that's all.'

'In other words, you are an invalid,' said Olivia, without trying to be tactful. She knew her father of old. He could be totally stubborn, even at the risk of cutting off his nose to spite his face.

'And d'you think I want everyone to know that?' he snapped shortly. 'It's all right for you, coming here and telling me what to do. I don't want anyone to see I can hardly stand, let alone walk!'

'I should think everyone knows that already,' replied Olivia practically. 'This is a small village, Dad. People know you. People care what happens to you.'

'Yes, well, I don't need their pity,' said her father, mopping at the trail of saliva that trickled from the paralysed side of his mouth. 'Nor yours, either,' he muttered. 'If that's all you've got to say to me, you can go.'

Olivia sighed. 'All right, all right. We won't talk about it.' She smoothed her palms over the knees of her trousers. 'I didn't come here to upset you.' She paused. 'Actually Jayne said you wanted to see me.'

'Hmmph.' The old man relaxed again. 'Well, why wouldn't I want to see my daughter? You're a sight for sore eyes, and that's a fact.'

Olivia smiled. 'Thank you.'

'Don't thank me. You were always the beauty of the family. And the brains, more's the pity!'

'Dad!'

'Well, you must know Linda and Martin are running the show around here while I'm—while I can't.' Olivia nodded, and he went on, 'So what do you think of their bright idea?'

Olivia frowned, not at all sure she ought to ask it, but doing so anyway. 'What bright idea?'

The door opening behind them and Linda bursting into the room drowned out any reply the old man might have made. 'Dad!' she exclaimed crossly. 'And Olivia. I thought you were in your room.' She turned back to her father. 'You know you're supposed to be resting. Anything you have to say to Olivia can wait until tomorrow, I'm sure.'

* * *

Olivia was up early the next morning. She'd had enough of being confined to the farm and she intended to catch the bus into Newcastle and spend the day doing some shopping. She also intended to find an agency and hire a car, though she kept that part of her plans to herself.

'Couldn't you get what you want in Chevingham?' Linda exclaimed, when she heard what her sister intended to do. 'Andy could give you a lift in the Land Rover. That would save you having to take the bus.'

'Thanks, but I prefer to go into Newcastle,' said Olivia politely, still feeling some resentment towards Linda for the way she'd behaved the night before. She'd acted as if Olivia had had no right to go and sit with her father. Not without clearing it with her first.

And, of course, any chance of further private conversation with him had been over. Although he'd protested, Linda had been adamant that he'd had enough visitors for one day. Olivia had only had time to squeeze his hand and tell him she'd see him later, before her sister had bustled her out of the room.

It was strange being back in the city after so many years had passed. It seemed so different, so modern, the alterations that had only been in the planning stage when she left now making the centre of town a vibrant, exciting place to visit.

She found a café and, after ordering an Americano, she took a seat in the window overlooking a shopping mall. It was a relief to be away from the farm and drinking a decent cup of coffee again. The instant brand Linda favoured was so bitter in comparison.

Revitalised, she left the café and spent some time exploring the shops. There were certainly plenty to choose from and, despite what Jayne had said, Olivia bought jeans and a couple of T-shirts, as well as a pair of combat boots to wear around the farm. The boots looked incongruous with the suede jacket and matching fringed skirt she'd worn to come to town, and she was laughing with the assistant when she looked through the shop window—straight into Joel Armstrong's eyes.

She couldn't help it. Her eyes widened and her breath caught somewhere in the back of her throat, so that when the assistant spoke again she found it very hard to answer her.

'Um—yes. Yes, I'll take them,' she said, knowing the girl was looking at her strangely. 'Thanks,' she added, quickly slipping her feet into the high-heeled pumps she'd taken off to try the boots on.

She was at the counter, paying for the boots with her credit card, when she became aware that Joel had entered the shop. It wasn't that he'd spoken to her or done anything to announce his presence; it was just a premonition she had that it was him.

It was madness but she could feel him near her, sensed the pressure of the air had changed since he came in. She wanted to turn and look at him, to ensure herself that she wasn't mistaken. God, she was going to be so disappointed if she was wrong.

But she wasn't wrong. When her purchase was completed and she could justifiably collect the bag containing her boots and turn around, he was there waiting for her. 'Hi,' he said as she crossed the shop towards him, and once again her stomach started its crazy plunge.

He looked so good, she thought helplessly. Even in a worn corded jacket with leather patches at the elbows, he looked big and dark and disturbingly familiar. His jeans hugged his legs, worn in places she knew she shouldn't be looking. And, goodness, she shouldn't be so glad to see him.

'Hi,' she answered in return, uncertain what to do next. 'Are you looking for shoes, too?'

'Do I look as if I need to?' he countered humorously as they stepped outside, drawing her eyes to the scuffed deck shoes he was wearing. 'No. You know I'm not.' His eyes skimmed her face. 'Are you on your own?'

Olivia nodded. 'Are you?'

'Until half-past two, when I've got to see one of my students,' he agreed, his warm breath fanning her cheek. 'Have you had lunch?'

Olivia swallowed. 'No.'

'So—d'you want to get a sandwich with me?'

There was nothing Olivia would have liked more, but she knew getting involved with Joel again was dangerous. She'd been sure she was so over him. Now she had goose-bumps just because he'd invited her to lunch.

'Well—I was going to see about renting a car,' she said lamely, and knew immediately from his expression that he wasn't fooled by her excuse.

'In other words, you'd rather not,' he said, lifting one shoulder dismissively. 'OK.' He paused. 'Some other time, perhaps.'

'No, wait!' As he would have turned away, she caught his sleeve and stopped him. 'I—I can see about renting a car after lunch. And I've got to eat. So—why not with you? If the offer's still good.'

Joel regarded her consideringly, wondering if he wouldn't be wiser to just call it a day. He still wasn't sure why he'd asked her, why he wanted to prolong what could only be an awkward interlude in his day.

'I get the feeling you're just humouring me,' he said, and her hand dropped quickly from his arm.

'I'm not.' Olivia's tongue circled her dry lips. 'I just didn't think it through, that's all.' She paused, and then added huskily, 'I didn't want you to feel—obliged to ask me.'

'Why would I feel that?'

He wasn't making it easy for her, and Olivia wondered now if he had had second thoughts. 'You know what I mean,' she said defensively.

Joel shook his head. 'I assume you mean because of what we once had.' His eyes darkened. He wouldn't let her humble him. 'Liv, I've told you already, I'm long past caring what you did or didn't do.'

Olivia wanted to scream. It wasn't fair, she thought. She'd done nothing wrong. Did he think she had no feelings at all?

But Joel wasn't finished. 'If you can't see I was only being civil,' he declared tersely, 'then perhaps we should just go our separate ways.'

Well, that was certainly telling her, he thought, refusing to back down. But, seeing the flush of colour that swept into her cheeks at his words, he couldn't help wondering why he felt this need to punish her. She'd inadvertently saved him from himself, hadn't she? He'd never have been satisfied with working at the farm permanently. And how could he have been able to afford four years at college if he'd had a wife and child to support?

'If that's what you want,' she said now, and in spite of himself, Joel couldn't let her go.

'It's not what I want,' he said between clenched teeth.

'For God's sake, I asked you, didn't I? I just never thought such a simple request would result in this inquisition.'

Olivia sighed. 'I'm sorry.'

So was Joel. But not for the same reason.

'So—where would you like to go?' she asked, and Joel jammed his balled fists into his pockets. *Bed*, he thought savagely, an insane image of Olivia spread-eagled on his sheets, her silky hair draped across his pillow, suddenly front and centre in his mind. 'It's very busy,' she went on. 'Do you think you'll have time?'

Another opportunity, but Joel didn't take it. 'How about buying a sandwich and eating it outdoors?' he suggested. 'Lots of people do that.'

'OK.'

She was annoyingly cooperative and as they walked to the nearby sandwich bar Joel reminded himself that he'd engineered this meeting, not her. He'd be far more convincing if he behaved pleasantly. Allowing her to bug him, to make him angry, would only convince her he wasn't as indifferent to her as he claimed.

CHAPTER FOUR

However, the nearby park was buzzing with young people. As well as there being nowhere to sit, Joel realised he had no desire to share the space with his own students.

He should have thought of that, he told himself irritably, turning his back on the open area with a feeling of frustration. Where now? he asked himself. And could only come up with one solution.

'Look, how do you feel about coming back to my office?' he suggested, and saw the way her eyes widened at his words.

'Your office?'

'My room at the university,' he explained abruptly. 'It's just a short walk from here.'

'All right.'

After a moment's pause, Olivia agreed, keeping any doubts she might have had about the advisability of doing such a thing to herself. After all, Joel couldn't have made his feelings any plainer. If she was suffering any pangs of memory they were hers alone.

The City University was one of the smaller places of learning. Concentrating mainly on computer technology,

it attracted students from all over the country as well as
some from further afield. It had an unparalleled reputation
and Joel never stopped feeling amazed that he'd been
accepted onto its faculty. There was even a certain amount
of satisfaction in taking Olivia there, even if he'd never
intended to do so.

His room was on the second floor, overlooking the
central courtyard. Below his windows, a quadrangle of
grass was surrounded by a cloistered walkway where
both lecturers and students could walk even on the
wettest days.

Predictably, Olivia walked straight across to the
windows, looking out with such concentration that Joel
wondered if she was estimating her chances should she
have to make her escape that way.

'Nice,' she said at last, turning and resting her hips on
the broad sill, and he didn't know whether she was refer-
ring to the view or to the generous proportions of his room.

'I'm glad you like it.' Joel unloaded the carrier containing the sandwiches and two bottles of mineral water onto
his desk. 'I have to admit, it took some getting used to.'

'What?' She left the window and came over to the desk.
'This room—or your appointment?'

'Both, I guess,' he said, with a wry smile. 'I was lucky.'

'Oh, I doubt that.' Deciding she might as well try and
relax, Olivia flopped down into the leather chair behind his
desk and swung it round in a full circle as a child might
do. 'I'm sure you're very good at your job.'

'Gee, thanks.' Joel was sardonic. 'Your approval means
a lot to me.'

Olivia pursed her lips. 'Don't be sarcastic!' she retorted,

and then, sensing he was laughing at her, she pulled a face. 'Anyway, what do you do?'

'Try to instil my love of technology into my students,' he replied, tearing open the sandwich wrappers.

'Is that all?'

Joel's brow ascended. 'Isn't it enough?' And when she continued to look at him, he said, 'Actually, I'm studying for a doctorate myself.'

'So you write, too?'

'Some.' Joel pushed the sandwiches towards her. 'Help yourself.'

Olivia reached for a bottle of water instead, unscrewing the cap and raising it to her lips. She was thirsty, she realised, or perhaps it was just being alone here with Joel that was making her mouth feel so dry.

'Tell me what you've written,' she said, watching as he pulled a sandwich out of its container and took a bite. She was trying to divert herself from noticing how strong and white his teeth looked against the undoubtedly sensual curve of his mouth. 'Could I have seen it?'

'Not unless you're into artificial intelligence,' responded Joel, swallowing rapidly. He studied his sandwich for a moment before continuing, 'I have had a couple of articles published in *Nerds Monthly*.'

Olivia stared at him 'You're making that up!' she exclaimed. 'I'm sure there's no such magazine.'

'Isn't there?'

He was evidently enjoying her confusion and she pulled a face. 'Joel—'

'OK, OK.' He finished his sandwich and reached for his own bottle of water. Then, before taking a drink, he added, 'They were in *Hot Key*, actually,' mentioning the name of an international computer publication that even Olivia had heard of.

'Fantastic,' she said applaudingly. 'Do you have copies?'

'I guess so.'

Joel was telling himself not to be seduced by her obvious admiration, but he couldn't help feeling impatient at his deliberate choice of verb. Dammit, they were talking, that was all. So why was he enjoying the sight of her sitting in his chair so damn much?

'Here?' she asked, looking about her.

'No, not here,' he replied flatly. 'At home.'

'Your home?' Olivia cradled her water bottle between her palms and regarded him curiously. 'Where do you live? In town?'

'Now, why would you want to know that?' Joel asked the question and then wished he hadn't. He was making too much of it. Before she could respond, he went on swiftly, 'I have a house in Millford. I bought it after Louise and I were divorced.'

'Louise?' Olivia said the name slowly. 'That would be your second wife?'

'Well, I haven't had a third. Yet.'

'Yet?' She picked up on that, as he'd known she would. 'Do you have someone in mind?'

'And if I had, do you think I'd tell you?' he countered smoothly. 'Eat your sandwich. It's getting warm.'

Olivia ignored his instruction, her tongue appearing briefly at the corner of her mouth. 'So—did you meet Louise at university?'

Joel sighed, wishing he'd never mentioned his ex-wife.

'I met her again when I went back to Bridgeford,' he said resignedly. 'After I'd got my degree.'

Olivia's jaw dropped. 'You don't mean to tell me you married Louise—*Webster*!'

'Why not?' Joel was defensive now. 'We always liked one another.'

'She liked you,' said Olivia with sudden vehemence. 'My God! Louise Webster. You used to say she was boring as hell!'

'I used to say a lot of things,' retorted Joel, pushing his other sandwich aside with a feeling of revulsion. 'And perhaps *boring* was what I wanted. I hadn't had a lot of success with anything else.'

Olivia glared at him for a few moments, her lips pursed mutinously, and then she pushed herself up from his chair and started towards the door. 'I knew I shouldn't have come here,' she said, and now Joel could hear a faint tremor in her voice. 'Thanks for the water. I find I'm not very hungry, after all.'

'Liv!' Despite the warning voice inside him that was telling him to let her go, Joel found himself taking the couple of strides necessary to put himself between her and the door. He leaned back against it. 'I'm sorry. I shouldn't have said that.'

'No, you shouldn't.'

Olivia halted uncertainly, her heart tripping over itself in its efforts to keep up with her hammering pulse. It wasn't just what he'd said that was making her heart race and causing the blood to rush madly through her veins. It was the painful realisation that she was jealous: jealous of his ex-wife, jealous of the child they'd had together, jealous of the success he'd made of his life once she was out of it.

'Look, why don't you go and sit down again and eat your sandwich?' he suggested gently, and something inside Olivia snapped.

'I'm not one of your bloody students,' she exploded, charging towards him with every intention of forcing him out of her way. 'You go and sit down. I'm leaving.'

Joel didn't move, however. He just lounged there against the door, lean and indolent, one ankle crossed over the other, apparently indifferent to her futile display. And, unless she wanted to grab his arm and try to drag him bodily away from the door, she had to stand there, feeling like an idiot, waiting for him to make the next move.

'What do you want me to say, Liv?' he asked suddenly, his voice lower, deeper, disturbingly sensual. He put out his hand, his lips twisting when she flinched, and plucked a silvery hair from the shoulder of her jacket. 'You and I know one another too well to indulge in this kind of lunacy. Does the fact that Louise and I got together annoy you? Is that why you're behaving like a spoiled brat?'

'You wish!'

But Olivia was panicking now. When he'd reached out, she'd been half afraid he was going to touch her cheek. And, conversely, now that he hadn't, she felt cheated. She'd wanted him to touch her, she wanted to feel those strong fingers stroking her heated flesh.

Oh, God!

'Just get out of my way, Joel,' she said, controlling the quiver in her voice with an effort.

'What if I don't want to?' he countered, and the breath she was taking caught somewhere in the back of her throat.

'Now who's being childish?' she panted. 'Be careful,

Joel, I'll begin to think you're the one who's got a problem. Why should I care who you chose to marry? I just hope you made her happier than you made me.'

Joel moved then. His hand grabbed her wrist, twisted it viciously behind her, forced her towards him whether she wanted it or not. 'Take that back,' he snarled, but Olivia was too stunned to do anything but gaze up at him with wide, startled eyes. 'Go on,' he persisted. 'Do it, or I'll break your bloody arm.'

Olivia blinked, and just like that the realisation that it was Joel who was holding her, Joel who was crushing her breasts against the rough lapels of his jacket, took all her fear away.

'You wouldn't do that, Joel,' she said, with amazing confidence in the circumstances. And although there was a heart-stopping moment when she thought she was wrong, finally, with a muffled oath, he thrust her away from him.

'No, I wouldn't,' he said hoarsely, stepping away from the door. 'I have more self-respect than that. Now—get out of here!'

Olivia hesitated. She knew that was what she should do. But she also knew that in some strange way the tables had been turned. Seeing the grim look on Joel's face as he waited for her to open the door, she sensed that, for all his harsh words, he wanted her out of there now just as much as she'd wanted to go a few minutes earlier.

But why?

It was an intriguing puzzle.

Was it only because he was angry with her for questioning his masculinity? Or had touching her disturbed him as much as it had disturbed her?

'What are you waiting for?'

He would have reached past her and jerked the door open then, but now Olivia put herself in his way. 'Joel,' she said huskily, moving towards him and grasping his forearms. 'We can't leave it like this.'

'Why not?'

He would have shaken himself free of her, but she was insistent, holding on to his arms, feeling the muscles bunch hard beneath her fingers. 'I thought we were friends, Joel,' she murmured, her thumb caressing the sleeve of his jacket. 'I'm not your enemy, you know.'

'This isn't going to work, Liv,' he warned, but she just gazed up at him with innocent green eyes.

'What isn't going to work?' she queried softly, and he growled deep in his throat.

'This,' he said savagely, gripping the back of her neck, pushing the silky shoulder-length hair aside, his fingers digging into her flesh. 'I should have known I couldn't trust you.'

Olivia opened her mouth to deny his claim, but the words were never spoken. With a muffled oath, Joel fastened his lips to hers, silencing anything but the moan of pleasure she couldn't quite restrain.

The kiss was deep and erotic, the sexual thrust of his tongue igniting all the raw, primitive emotions she'd suppressed for so long. She wanted him with an urgency that defied rhyme or reason, sinking into him completely, hazed by desire.

Without her hardly being aware of it, her arms were around his neck and he was moving her back against the door behind her, leaning into her sensually, his hands burning her hips. She only realised he'd rucked her skirt above her knees and parted her legs with his thigh when she felt the cool air upon her skin.

His mouth ate at hers, bruised the soft flesh, left her weak and trembling beneath the weight of his body as he leant against her. She could feel every part of him, feel every bone and angle. And every unguarded muscle, so that when the pressure against her stomach became unmistakable, she put down a hand and caressed his length through the taut fabric of his jeans.

She heard him say an oath thickly, and then he was tipping her jacket off her shoulders, tearing open her blouse so he could press open-mouthed kisses between her breasts. His palms pressed against the taut nipples swelling against her half-bra, his fingers rough against her soft skin.

He groaned and she felt an answering pain deep in her belly. There was a pulse throbbing between her legs and she knew she was already wet. When his hand dropped lower, cradled her thigh, before moving round to probe beneath the thin silk of her thong, she let out a moan of protest. But she didn't try to stop him. She honestly didn't think she had the strength.

'Dear God, Joel,' she whispered unsteadily, wondering if he intended to take her there against the door of his office. It was possible. She was certainly making it easy for him. Like some cheap tart, an inner voice taunted, and suddenly she felt sick. Had she really sunk that low?

Thankfully, it wasn't a question she had to answer. Whether Joel would have unzipped his jeans and pushed himself into her hot, wet heat became a moot point when someone knocked at the door.

They both froze, and Joel at least was reminded of a

similar occasion when they were both still at school. Then, they'd arranged to meet in her father's loft and, like now, things had rapidly got out of hand. Until Ben Foley had come into the barn…

Predictably, it wasn't something he wanted to remember at this moment. Dammit, he thought, he'd sworn Olivia would never get under his skin again. And now here he was, caught like some guilty schoolboy, the only difference being he was still wearing his trousers.

Olivia was the first to recover. Scrambling out from under him, she scooped her jacket off the floor and put it on. Dragging the two sides together over her unbuttoned blouse, she reached for her bag.

'Aren't you going to answer it?' she hissed, checking that her skirt didn't look too creased. It did, of course, and she was sure anyone with half an eye would know what they'd been doing. But there was nothing she could do about it. She was fairly sure she hadn't a scrap of make-up left on her face.

Joel extended his arms and pushed himself away from the door with an effort. He'd sagged against the panels when she'd moved, reluctant to display the treacherous evidence of his need. God, he realised, feeling dazed, it was half-past two already. It would be Cheryl Brooks, ready and eager to discuss the finer points of binary calculus.

He was so screwed, he thought dully, or rather he wasn't. He flexed his shoulders and straightened, turning to regard Olivia through narrowed eyes. He should be grateful for the interruption, so why was he feeling so frustrated? But heaven help him, he could feel Olivia's essence on his fingers, was still breathing the potent scent of her arousal into his lungs.

She was getting agitated. He could see it. She arched her

brows, nodding pointedly towards the door, showing him in every way she could without speaking again that he should see who it was. Joel felt his lips twitch in spite of himself. Would she still be as eager when she saw Cheryl was his visitor?

'OK, OK,' he mouthed, running slightly unsteady fingers through his hair, checking there were no tell-tale signs to betray him. Then, turning, he reached for the handle. Without further ado, he opened the door.

Olivia tensed. She couldn't help it. Whoever it was, she had no desire to stay and be introduced. She wanted out of there, immediately. Her senses had cooled now and she was appalled at the way she'd behaved.

The girl waiting outside only looked to be about eighteen, but she was probably older. It hadn't occurred to Olivia before now that Joel would have female students as well as male and the knowledge disturbed her. The girl had long blonde hair, worn over one shoulder, her tight jeans and cropped top accentuating her youthful appearance.

'Hi, Joel,' she said, proving their relationship was fairly familiar. Then she saw Olivia and the smile she'd been wearing faded.

'Cheryl,' Joel said feebly, aware that he wasn't quite up to this. He glanced at his watch. 'You're early.'

'Just five minutes,' Cheryl protested, and Olivia could tell she wasn't suited either. She'd probably been looking forward to a cosy tête-à-tête with her professor, and now Olivia had spoiled the mood.

'Yeah, right.' Joel glanced briefly at Olivia and then back at his visitor. 'Well, why don't you come in? Um— Mrs Garvey was just leaving.'

CHAPTER FIVE

THE next couple of days passed without incident and, waking up one morning, Olivia realised it was almost a week since she'd arrived at Blades Farm. How long was she going to stay? she wondered. She had planned for this to be just a flying visit. But somehow now she was in no hurry to get back to London and Linda hadn't mentioned anything about when she was going to leave.

There had been a little animosity when she'd arrived back from Newcastle driving a small Renault from the rental agency. But it had soon blown over and Olivia was finding the sense of freedom having her own transport gave her well worth any unpleasantness from her brother-in-law. Besides, it enabled her to get out and see something of the area she'd grown up in, and she had every intention of persuading her father to join her. Eventually.

The car had even helped to put her encounter with Joel to the back of her mind. She hadn't forgotten what had happened. How could she? And sometimes, particularly at night, she'd wake up and find her breasts tingling and a moist place between her legs.

But she'd get over it. The pangs of frustration she was

feeling were just her body reminding her that she was still a young woman with a young woman's sexual needs. During her marriage to Bruce she'd had to stifle those needs, and it was unfortunate that it had been Joel who'd aroused them again.

But any attractive man would have done, she assured herself fiercely, flinging back the duvet and swinging her legs over the side of the bed. It was her misfortune that she'd let Joel get close enough to stir emotions she'd kept in check for the better part of six years.

And remembering how their encounter had ended, she felt again the surge of resentment that had filled her when he'd dismissed her. OK, she'd been planning to leave—desperate to get out of there, actually—but had he had to make her feel as if she'd been just another drain on his precious time?

She breathed deeply, refusing to let thoughts of Joel ruin her day. She'd seen him, they'd talked, and now she didn't care if she didn't see him again. Let him make eyes at his adoring students. The female ones, of course.

For once the bathroom was empty, and, aware that there were no guarantees that that state of affairs would continue, Olivia quickly washed and cleaned her teeth. Promising herself a more thorough inspection later, she returned to her room and dressed in jeans and a T-shirt, her only concession to style the scarlet chiffon scarf she knotted about her neck.

Downstairs, she found her sister in the kitchen, loading the dishwasher, the crumbs and dirty dishes from breakfast still littering the table.

'Let me do that,' said Olivia at once, but Linda merely shook her head.

'Don't be silly,' she said, her glance saying that, even in the stone-washed jeans and cotton T-shirt, Olivia looked over-dressed. 'There's coffee on the stove. Help yourself.'

'Has Dad had his breakfast?' asked Olivia, doing as Linda had suggested. She took a sip of the coffee and stifled a grimace. 'I'll go and see how he is, shall I?'

'He's resting,' said Linda, as she said every morning. So far, Olivia had been unable to repeat the occasion when she and her father had had a chance to talk alone together. 'D'you want some toast?'

'I'll get it.'

Olivia refused to let her sister wait on her, and, taking the cut loaf out of the stone barrel, she extracted a slice and popped it in the toaster. Then, tucking the tips of her fingers into the back pockets of her jeans, she added, 'Haven't you ever thought of getting Dad a wheelchair?'

It was the first time she'd mentioned it to Linda, hoping against hope that she'd have another chance to speak to her father about it. But beggars couldn't be choosers and she was determined to get him out of the house.

Linda stared at her now. 'A wheelchair!' she echoed disparagingly. 'You can't think Dad would ever use a wheelchair!'

'Why not?'

'You know why not.' Linda returned to her task. 'He's far too independent.'

'He's not very independent, stuck in that room all the time,' retorted Olivia steadily. 'It would do him good to get some fresh air.'

Linda shook her head. 'I suppose that's why you insisted on hiring that car, is it?'

'No—'

'You didn't think we might have tried to get him out in the Land Rover or his old Saab?'

Olivia could feel herself weakening, but she stood her ground. 'And have you?'

Now it was Linda's turn to look defensive. 'What would be the point? I've told you, Dad will go out when he can do so under his own steam and not before.'

'And when will that be?'

'Who knows?' Linda's voice had sharpened. 'Nurse Franklin comes in every week to help him with his physical therapy. Perhaps you ought to ask her. Though I have to tell you, you're wasting your time.'

Olivia heard the bread pop out of the toaster and was grateful for the opportunity to have something else to do. Buttering the slice with a knife she found on the table, she helped herself to a smear of marmalade before taking a bite.

'Anyway, I wanted to talk to you,' said Linda with a distinct change of tone. She closed the dishwasher and switched it on. 'Martin's gone into Chevingham, but he'll be back about half-past ten. Maybe we could all have coffee together?'

Olivia kept her eyes fixed on the slice of toast she was holding, wondering what had brought this on. In the week since her arrival, she and Martin had barely said more than a dozen words to one another. She couldn't imagine him wanting to sit down and share morning coffee with someone he evidently despised.

Unless...

She recalled suddenly the silk camisole she'd given to Jayne. Had they found out about that? And if so was she to bear the brunt of their joint displeasure? Had Linda decided she needed her husband's support on this occasion?

'Um—well, I was thinking of going out,' she murmured awkwardly, even though what she'd really been hoping to do was spend a little more time with her father. With or without Linda's chaperonage.

'I see.' Linda stood at the other side of the scrubbed pine table, regarding her coldly. 'Oh, well, don't let us stop you. Not if you'd prefer to go out.'

Olivia sighed. Perversely now, she felt ashamed. They were trying to be friendly, and she was throwing their kindness back in their faces.

'No,' she declared firmly. 'I can go out any time. What do you want to talk about, anyway? I hope I haven't done anything wrong.'

'Heavens, no.' Linda was all smiles now. 'It's just—well, you've been here a week now and you've got some idea of the way the farm works. Martin and I have come up with an idea that we'd like to put to you. But I'd rather wait until he's here to explain it to you himself.'

In spite of her misgivings, Olivia was intrigued. Was this anything to do with what her father had started to tell her when Linda had burst in on them the other evening? He had definitely mentioned some idea his daughter and son-in-law had had. Was she to find out what it was from an entirely unexpected source?

The time between her agreeing to listen to what they had to say and Martin's return dragged. Having checked that her father was indeed sleeping and therefore unable to be disturbed, Olivia decided to go for a walk. She had over an hour before the half-past-ten deadline, and it was a pleasant morning. Collecting her boots and a jacket from upstairs, she let herself out of the front door and walked briskly away from the house.

She had no particular direction in mind. Just a need to escape Linda's overpowering presence. Despite being a pushover where her husband was concerned, Linda certainly liked to throw her weight around with the other members of the household.

Avoiding the immediate environs of the house for fear Linda would see her, Olivia skirted the trees that screened the paddock and made her way across the stockyard to the barn. There were chickens running loose here and even a couple of geese that hissed alarmingly. But Olivia wasn't troubled. It was amazing how the memories of childhood came flooding back.

She could see her nephew in the distance. Andy was up on a ladder, apparently painting one of the cottages that housed the families of the men who worked on the farm. Which was odd, she reflected, frowning. The tenants usually looked after the cottages themselves.

Perhaps he wasn't painting, she thought, dodging into the barn so he wouldn't think she was spying on him. He could just be repairing the guttering. Or cleaning the windows—but that wasn't likely either.

The barn was familiar. Although she would have preferred not to think about it, this was where she and Joel had used to meet after school. There'd been a loft, fragrant with the heat of the sun on the hay her father had stored there. It had been their own private hideaway—though she guessed now that her father had known exactly what was going on.

The ladder leading up into the loft was still there and,

after assuring herself that she was alone, Olivia couldn't resist climbing it. For old times' sake, she told herself firmly. To see if anything had changed.

However, as she started up, she heard a rustle in the straw and she stiffened instinctively. Rats? she wondered uneasily. Or just a bird that had taken up residence in the roof. She sighed. Was she really going to let anything, bird or animal, frighten her away? Whatever it was, it would be far more frightened of her.

She continued up, listening hard for any other sound, but she heard nothing. All the same, when she stuck her head above the hatch, she knew a moment's apprehension. She'd seen enough horror films to be able to imagine the worst.

But all appeared to be as it should be and she started down again. Only to come to an abrupt halt when she heard something scrape across the floor above her head. That was no bird, she thought. No rat, either. Her fingers tightened on the rungs of the ladder. She ought to go and report what she'd heard to Andy or one of the other men.

But, come to think of it, she hadn't seen any other men about the farm. Of course, she hadn't spent much time on the farm since she'd come back, so perhaps that wasn't so surprising. And calling Andy seemed like such a feeble thing to do. Who could be up there? Wouldn't they have tackled her sooner if they'd intended her any harm?

It was nerve-racking but, steeling herself, she started up again. 'Hello there,' she called, giving whoever it was plenty of warning if they wanted to escape. She seemed to remember there was a gantry at the other side of the loft where the hay had been loaded. It was at least an eight-foot jump to the ground, but if the intruder was desperate...

Once again she reached the hatch, but this time she climbed up into the loft. It had occurred to her that it might be kids. What an ideal place to bunk off school.

Olivia looked about her. 'I know there's somebody here,' she said, trying to see beyond the tumbled bales of hay into the shadowy corners of the loft. 'If you don't come out, I'll—I'll—' she had a spurt of inspiration '—I'll go and fetch one of the geese to find you.'

Not that that was remotely likely, she acknowledged. Although she wasn't afraid to cross the yard, she doubted she'd have the guts to pick up one of the geese. But, hopefully, a kid might not know that. Particularly one who wasn't familiar with birds or animals.

There was no movement, however, and Olivia sighed. 'OK,' she said. 'If that's what you want.' She pretended to take hold of the ladder. 'I'll be back—'

'No, wait!'

The voice was definitely that of a child's, she thought with some relief. It had occurred to her that some vagrant might have spent the night in the barn. But, as she watched, a boy detached himself from the pile of sacks where he'd been hiding. A tall boy, but not much more than eleven years old, she thought.

He stood beside the sacks for a moment, his face in shadow, only his eyes reflecting the light. Blue eyes, Olivia saw; resigned yet mutinous. As if he'd been expecting someone to come looking for him, but that didn't mean he had to like it.

'Hi,' said Olivia after a moment. 'You do realise you're trespassing, don't you?'

'How do you know?' he demanded, and she realised she

didn't. Could he possibly belong to one of the families who lived on the farm?

'What's your name?' she asked, but this time he didn't answer her. 'You don't live on the farm, do you? You might as well tell me. I'm going to find out anyhow.'

The boy's chin jutted. 'No, I don't live on the farm,' he admitted at last. 'I wish I did. Anything would be better than living with my mum and the hulk!'

Olivia gasped. 'Don't call your father the hulk!'

'He's not my father,' retorted the boy at once, and Olivia felt a glimmer of understanding. Obviously his parents were separated, and he wasn't happy with the arrangement.

'All the same,' she said, trying to think of something positive to say, 'I expect they'll be worried about you. Shouldn't you be in school?'

The boy shrugged, which she assumed was a yes, and leaned down to grab the handle of a backpack lying on the floor. As he did so, a ray of sunlight streaming through a crack in the wall illuminated his thin features, and Olivia felt her heart turn over.

'What's your name?' she asked again, though she was fairly sure she knew his surname. Goodness! She moistened her dry lips. He had to be Joel's son. And it all fit, she realised. Him, living with his mother; his parents separated—*divorced*! The only thing Joel hadn't told her was that Louise had married again.

'Sean,' the boy muttered now, completing his identity. 'What's yours?'

'Olivia. Olivia—Foley.' She used the name deliberately, guessing he would know who owned the farm.

He regarded her defiantly. 'Are you going to tell Mum where I am?'

Olivia sighed. 'I've got to. I can't leave you here. How long have you been up here anyway? What time did you leave for school?'

'I didn't,' said Sean, low-voiced, and Olivia stared at him in disbelief.

'Oh, no!' she exclaimed. 'Don't tell me you've been up here all night?'

Once again, Sean didn't answer her, and she was left to fill the gaps herself. His mother must be desperate by this time. Losing a child was every parent's nightmare.

'I must tell your mother you're safe,' she said gently. 'What's her name?' Not Armstrong, obviously. 'Where do you live?'

'I'd rather you told Dad,' said Sean miserably, and once again Olivia's heart flipped a beat.

'Why?' she ventured, aware that it wasn't really anything to do with her, but assuring herself she was only trying to make sense of his answer.

'Cos he didn't believe me last time,' the boy declared obliquely. 'I told him I didn't want to live with Mum and—and Stewart.'

'Stewart?' Olivia was fishing, and Sean took the bait.

'Stewart Barlow,' he said without thinking, instantly supplying the one name she didn't have.

Olivia absorbed this without saying anything, aware that Sean was regarding her with hopeful eyes. 'Will you speak to my dad?' he asked, twisting the strap of his backpack round his thin wrist. 'Honestly, he won't be mad at you if you don't tell Mum first.'

Olivia tucked her thumbs into the back pockets of her jeans. 'So what's your dad's name?' she asked, realising she wasn't supposed to know who he was.

'It's Armstrong,' said Sean much more cheerfully. 'Joel Armstrong. He's a teacher,' he added, as if that carried more weight.

A quiver of apprehension ran down Olivia's spine and she shivered. She could hardly believe she was standing here, talking to Joel's son, trying to decide what was best for the boy. She was fairly sure Joel wouldn't like the idea of her being involved in his private affairs. But, in spite of that, she couldn't deny a tremor of excitement at the power Sean had inadvertently given her.

'Where do you live, Sean?' she asked again, and the boy's eyes narrowed.

'You're not going to tell my mum, are you?' he blurted. 'Oh, please, I don't want to live with them any more.'

'Why not?' Olivia frowned. 'They don't—well, they don't hurt you, do they?'

'No.' Sean was sulky. 'I just don't like my stepfather, that's all.'

Olivia considered. Bearing in mind her own feelings about Martin Dempsey, she could sympathise. But Sean was too young to make that kind of decision for himself. 'Why don't you live with your father, then?' she asked. 'You like him, don't you?'

'Oh, yes!' Sean's face lit up. Then he hunched his shoulders as reality kicked in. 'But he works at the university in Newcastle. Besides, Mum said I needed two parents, not just one.'

'I see.' Olivia was beginning to understand the situation.

'But Stewart's not my parent!' exclaimed Sean, his expression darkening with frustration. He broke off and looked at her, waiting for her to say something. 'Please, don't tell my mum.'

'Tell me where you live and I'll think about it,' replied Olivia cautiously, and Sean expelled a heavy sigh.

'Twenty-six Church Close,' he muttered unwillingly. 'But she won't be there. She'll be at work.'

Olivia doubted Louise would be at work if she knew her son was missing. In the same situation, Olivia knew she'd have been doing everything in her power to find out where he'd gone. 'Church Close?' she said. 'Is that in Bridgeford?'

Sean nodded. 'It's one of the new houses behind the church.'

'Ah.'

'It's a horrible place. I don't like it,' he added vehemently. 'My dad's house is much nicer. And it's bigger, too.'

'Is it?' Olivia accepted his assessment, but she couldn't help thinking it was the people who occupied the houses, not the houses themselves, that were determining his opinion. 'OK,' she said at last, deciding she owed Louise no favours. 'I'll ring your father.' But when his face cleared, she went on warningly, 'Be prepared. He probably knows all about the fact that you're missing by now.'

CHAPTER SIX

JOEL was in the library at the university, doing some research for a paper he was writing, when his mobile phone trilled.

Immediately, half the eyes in the room turned in his direction and he made an open-handed gesture of apology as he reached to turn the phone off. Whoever it was would have to wait until he finished what he was doing, he thought impatiently. Certainly none of his colleagues would think of disturbing him here.

But he couldn't help noticing the number being displayed as he flipped the mobile open. It was unfamiliar to him and conversely that troubled him. He was remembering what had happened a few days ago, and, although he had no reason to suspect this call had anything to do with his son, he gritted his teeth and pressed the button to connect the call.

'Yeah,' he muttered, barely audibly, though the pained looks he was receiving proved he wasn't fooling anybody. Stifling an oath, he gathered his papers together and thrust them one-handed into his case, quitting the room with ill grace.

'Joel?'

Bloody hell, it was Olivia. Joel thought he'd have recognised her voice even in his sleep, but that didn't make
him feel any the less aggressive at having to take her call.

'What do you want, Liv?' he demanded, and even to his
own ears he sounded belligerent. He half expected her to
make some biting comment and ring off.

But she didn't. With creditable coolness, she said,
'There's someone here who wants to speak to you, Joel,'
and a moment later a timid voice said,

'It's me, Dad,' and he knew he hadn't been wrong in an-
ticipating trouble.

'Sean!' he exclaimed. 'Hell's bells, why aren't you in
school?'

'Because I'm not,' said Sean defensively. 'Can I come
and see you?'

Joel sagged back against the wall outside the library,
dropping his book bag at his feet, raking impatient fingers
through his hair. 'Sean, I'm at the university. I've got a
lecture in—' he consulted his watch '—in exactly forty-five
minutes. I don't have time to see you now.'

Sean made no response to this but Joel heard a muffled
exchange going on in the background. And as he listened,
he realised something that he should have questioned right
away. Sean was talking to *Olivia*! How had *that* happened?

'Sean,' he said sharply, resenting the fact that he couldn't
hear what they were saying. 'Sean, where are you?'

There was another pause, while frustration welled up
inside him, and then Olivia spoke again. 'I'd have thought
you'd have had the grace to abandon your lectures while
your son was missing,' she said accusingly, and Joel felt
as if the ground had just opened up beneath his feet.

'What did you say?' he asked harshly, but he already knew what she meant.

'Sean didn't go home last night,' said Olivia flatly. 'Don't pretend you don't know.'

'I don't. Or rather I didn't!' exclaimed Joel, trying desperately to get a handle on the situation. 'What do you mean, he didn't go home? How do you know? Did Louise tell you?'

'Louise, no.' Olivia sounded impatient. 'I haven't spoken to Louise. Sean told me. And he insisted on me calling you first.'

'Damn!' Joel pushed himself away from the wall, unable to control his agitation. 'So how long has he been with you?'

'Well, not all night, obviously,' retorted Olivia crisply. She paused. 'I—found him in the barn about an hour ago.'

'The barn?'

'Yes, the barn. In the loft, actually. I suppose that was why no one knew he was there.'

Joel groaned. Unwillingly the memory of their meetings, their lovemaking, in the loft came back to haunt him again. But evidently Olivia had no such sensibilities.

'He apparently spent the night there,' she continued evenly. 'What I can't understand is how you didn't know he was missing.'

Joel could have told her. It was obvious that when—*if*—Louise had discovered her son's disappearance, she'd immediately assumed that once again he'd sought refuge with his father. But he hadn't, and Joel's blood ran cold at the thought of what could have happened to the boy.

'Did he tell you this is the second time he's run away in less than a week?' he asked, though it was hardly an explanation.

'No.' There was another brief silence while Olivia absorbed this. Then, 'Are you saying he came to the university to find you?' and Joel blew out a weary breath.

'To my house in Millford, actually,' he said tersely. 'Now do you see why I might not have been told what was going on?'

'I'm beginning to,' she answered. And then, in an entirely different tone, 'What do you want me to do? Take him home?'

Joel heard Sean's vehement protests that she'd promised he could see his father and made an immediate decision. 'Do you think you could bring him to Millford?' he asked, aware he was going to have to get someone to cover his lecture. 'I know it's an imposition, but I could meet you there in—say, forty minutes?'

Another pause, shorter this time, before Olivia said, 'I could do that.' She took a breath. 'OK. Sean can give me directions. We'll see you in about three-quarters of an hour.'

Although she knew Linda wouldn't be very pleased that her plans were being disrupted, Olivia didn't tell her what was going on. She guessed if Linda found out that Joel's son had spent the night in the barn, she would insist on informing his mother. And while that was possibly the most sensible thing to do, if Louise was worried about her son, why hadn't she been going from door to door, asking if anyone had seen him?

Fortunately, Martin hadn't come back yet so Olivia was able to collect her keys and unlock the rental car without incident. All the same, after reversing up to the barn and telling Sean to jump in the back and keep his head down, she felt absurdly guilty. This wasn't her problem and she was all kinds of a fool for getting involved.

It was still too early when they arrived at Joel's house, but Olivia was happy to be away from Bridgeford. She knew no one in Millford; hoped no one would recognise her. And, besides, it gave her a little more time to talk to Sean.

Joel's house overlooked the village green; an elegant Georgian structure, it had windows on either side of an oak door, with a distinctive fanlight above. What had once been a coach-house now served as a garage, Sean told her. He obviously liked being her guide and proudly showed her round to the back.

There was a football lying on the lawn and Sean immediately dropped his backpack onto the patio and started kicking the ball around. 'Can you play football?' he asked, seeing her watching him, and Olivia shook her head.

'You've got to be kidding,' she said, laughing. 'I've got two left feet.'

'What does that mean? Two left feet?' Sean looked puzzled.

'It means I'm no good at sports,' explained Olivia wryly. 'I go running instead. That doesn't need any skill at all.'

Sean started heading the ball. 'Where do you run? Around the farm?'

'No.' Olivia realised she hadn't had any exercise since she'd arrived in Bridgeford. 'I used to live in New York. I did all my running there.'

Sean stopped what he was doing and stared at her. 'New York,' he echoed. 'That's in America, isn't it?'

'Yes. Have you been there?'

'Not to New York,' said Sean seriously. 'But Dad took me to Disneyworld last year. That's in Florida,' he added, in case she didn't understand, and Olivia made an admiring face.

'Cool,' she said. 'And did you enjoy it?'

'Oh, yeah.' Sean picked up the ball, cradling it in his arms. 'It was great.' He grimaced. 'Stewart doesn't like holidays. Not unless he can play golf all the time.'

Olivia bit her lip, not wanting to get into family politics. 'Do you play golf?' she asked instead, hoping to divert him. 'My—my ex-husband was very keen.'

'You were married?' Sean gazed at her. 'Was that when you lived in America?'

'I—Yes.' She glanced about her. 'Do you come here a lot?'

It was the wrong thing to say. She knew that as soon as Sean's lips turned down. 'Hardly at all,' he muttered gloomily. 'Just some weekends, that's all.'

'That sounds like quite a lot to me,' said Olivia cheerfully. 'So what do you and your dad do? Go to football matches, that sort of thing?'

'Sometimes,' admitted Sean, still looking dejected. 'Do you think he'll be long?'

Realising Joel's arrival was playing on the boy's mind, too, Olivia endeavoured to distract him. 'Tell me about when you went to Florida. Did you see any alligators?'

Sean brightened at once. 'Oh, yeah,' he said. 'When we stayed in Miami, we went on a trip into the Everglades. We went on one of those hover-boats. It was really exciting.'

'You mean an airboat,' said Olivia, nodding. 'Mmm, I've been on one of those, too. They go really fast, don't they?'

'They're awesome,' said Sean, with boyish enthusiasm. 'Dad says we can go back some time and do it again.'

'Hey, well, that's something to look forward to,' said Olivia, hoping to sustain the mood, but Sean hunched his shoulders now.

'Holidays aren't very long,' he muttered. 'I want to live with my dad. Not just see him now and then.'

Olivia sighed. 'I'm sure you love your mother, too,' she said. 'How would she feel if you lived with your father?'

'She wouldn't care,' said Sean sulkily. 'So long as she's got Stewart and—and—'

'And who?'

'Nobody.' Sean scowled. 'Do you think I should go and look for Dad's car?'

Olivia frowned, but she couldn't think of any reason why not, and, nodding, she let him go. But she sensed he had something on his mind, something more than just his eagerness to be with his father. Could his stepfather have anything to do with it? She didn't want to think so, but there was something he wasn't telling her. Perhaps he'd tell his father. After all, she told herself again, it wasn't her problem.

Following Sean round to the front of the property, she was just in time to see Joel's Lexus pull to a halt at the gate. He thrust open his door and got out and, despite everything, her heart quickened and her mouth went dry.

He was so attractive, she though painfully. Even now, in khaki cargo pants and a cream chambray shirt, the neck open to reveal the brown column of his throat, he looked dark and disturbingly male. Despite the worried expression marring his deeply tanned features, he was strikingly familiar. Big and strong, coiled strength and brooding grey eyes. Heavens, no wonder she'd behaved so outrageously in his office at the university. Just looking at him now, she felt her palms dampen and her body begin to heat.

Sean hesitated a moment and then ran back around the

house and Olivia wondered if he thought his father's grim expression was solely directed at him. She didn't kid herself. Her involvement hadn't gone unnoticed. Joel might be grateful to her for bringing the boy here, but he was probably resenting every moment of it.

If Joel wondered why his son should have run away, he didn't show it, and Olivia shifted a little nervously as he slammed the car door and strode through the wrought-iron gate that footed the garden path. But she refused to scurry away like a scared rabbit. She found she cared too much about Sean to do that.

Joel's eyes found hers and she steeled herself to face his censure. But all he said was, 'Thanks for bringing him here, Liv. God knows what he might have done if you hadn't found him when you did.'

Olivia managed a careless shrug. 'What do you think he'd have done?' she asked, stepping out of his way.

'Found his way here. I hope,' said Joel fervently. 'As he did a few days ago.' He shook his head, looking along the path his son had taken. 'Crazy kid! What the hell am I going to do about him?'

Olivia took an unsteady breath. 'He wants to be with you,' she said, aware as she did so that she knew exactly how Sean felt. Being with Joel again was reminding her of how it had been when they were together. Despite what he'd done to her, she still had feelings for this man.

'And how am I supposed to handle that?' Joel pushed agitated fingers through his hair. 'Dammit, I agreed that he should live with Louise and Stewart. I thought their situation was a more normal one for an impressionable child.'

'Stewart's not his father,' said Olivia, unable to ignore

his anxiety. She paused. 'How old was Sean when you—well, when you and your wife split up?'

'Six,' said Joel tersely. 'But the marriage hadn't worked for ages. Louise and I were already living separate lives.'

'Stewart,' said Olivia, understanding, and when Joel nodded in assent she badly wanted to put her arms around him and comfort him.

But that was too much, even for her. Swallowing, she pushed a hand into the front pocket of her jeans and pulled out her keys. 'Well, I'll leave you to it,' she said, with enforced lightness. 'Don't be too hard on him. He's a good kid.'

'I'm glad you think so.' Disturbingly, Joel's voice had thickened and she found she couldn't look away from his searching gaze. 'He should have been our son, Liv,' he muttered fiercely. 'Yours—and mine.'

Olivia felt a quiver of awareness sweep over her. The intimacy of the moment, his nearness and the bone-deep remembrance of all they'd shared—and lost—was turning her legs to jelly. For a moment she couldn't move, frozen by the force of words that tore her composure to shreds. The desire to reach out to him was almost overwhelming, but then, as if regretting his own weakness—or had she only imagined it?—Joel inclined his head.

'Thanks again for looking after him,' he said stiffly. 'I appreciate it.'

'You're not going!'

Unnoticed, Sean had ventured back along the path, probably wondering what was taking so long, Olivia reflected tensely. He had the football in his arms again, clutched to his thin chest like a talisman, his blue eyes round and filled with concern.

'Mrs Garvey's got to get back,' said Joel at once, going towards him. As he passed her, Olivia's nostrils were assailed by the mingled scents of soap and man, but her response was arrested by the indignant expression on Sean's face.

'You said your name was Olivia Foley!' he exclaimed, proving he hadn't forgotten their conversation. 'You said you lived at the farm.'

Olivia didn't remember saying that, but she understood his confusion. 'My name is Foley,' she told him. 'It used to be Garvey, but I changed back to my old name last year.'

'When you got a divorce,' said Sean, turning triumphantly to his father. 'You see. I knew I was right.'

'Well, it's good to be right about something,' remarked Joel drily, still angry with himself for confronting Olivia. 'So—let's go indoors and you can tell me why you ran away. Again.'

'Can she come, too?'

Evidently Sean had decided he needed some support, but all Olivia wanted to do was get away. 'I can't, Sean,' she said, hating having to disappoint him. 'You talk to your father; I'm sure he'll understand how you feel.'

She was forced to look at Joel then, willing him to reinforce what she was saying, but conversely, Joel didn't immediately respond. He could see Sean had taken a liking to Olivia and, while that ought not to please him, the temptation to have a woman's angle had to outweigh his own feelings towards her.

'You can stay if you like,' he said offhandedly, half hoping she'd turn him down. At least, if she did, Sean couldn't blame him for her decision. God, he thought in-

credulously, was he really pandering to the boy after the
way he'd behaved?

'Oh, well, I—'

'Please!' Sean came forward now and touched her
sleeve. 'I want to show you my room.'

Olivia shook her head, but it wasn't an indication of
what she was thinking. 'I'm sure your father would rather
have you to himself,' she said, glancing at Joel's taut face
for a moment. 'Wouldn't you?'

Joel's jaw tightened. 'Stay and have coffee at least,' he
said carelessly, but Olivia knew he was deliberately forcing
her to make the decision.

'O—K,' she said, unable to resist smiling into Sean's
relieved face. 'Now, you're not going to take that football
into the house, are you?'

CHAPTER SEVEN

JOEL had no real idea how he felt as he fished his keys out of his pocket and opened the door to his home.

Despite the fact that he hadn't lived like a monk in the years since his second divorce, he'd never brought a woman to his house before. And the fact that it was Olivia made it all the more unsettling. He didn't want her here; didn't want the certain knowledge that after she'd gone, he'd still feel her presence. But it was too late now.

Beyond the heavy door, a square entrance hall gave access to the main rooms of the house. A polished parquet floor was spread with a couple of colourful rugs he'd picked up on a trip to India, and a carved oak chest sat at the foot of a curved staircase.

Joel closed the door and Olivia concentrated on her surroundings. That way, she hoped, she wouldn't reflect on the fact that apart from Sean they were alone here.

And it was easy to admire the high-ceilinged rooms she glimpsed as Joel led the way to the kitchen. Without the obvious financial restrictions they'd had when they were married, he'd proved he had excellent taste. The mix of ancient and modern, of different textures and subtle colours, was exactly what the old house had needed.

'I'm hungry,' said Sean at once, opening the fridge with the familiarity of long use and looking inside. 'Can I have some cheese, Dad?'

'I suppose so.' Joel had gone immediately to fill the filter with coffee, but now he glanced over his shoulder with a resigned expression. 'Don't they feed you at Church Close?'

Sean's face darkened. 'Yes,' he muttered sulkily. 'But I haven't had any breakfast.'

'And whose fault is that?' retorted his father at once and Olivia closed her eyes for a moment, knowing that was exactly the wrong attitude to take with his son.

'Mine, I suppose,' blurted Sean, and she was sure there were tears in his eyes when he dropped the unopened cheese onto the counter and charged out of the room. They heard his footsteps thundering up the stairs and then the distinctive thud of a slamming door.

Joel hunched his shoulders and turned from what he was doing to rest his hips against the fitted unit. Then, looking absurdly like his son, he exclaimed, 'Now what did I say?'

'You know what you said,' Olivia told him evenly. 'Be a bit more understanding, can't you? He's very —fragile right now.'

Joel snorted. 'And you'd know this, how? Or have you a growing family I know nothing about?'

Olivia propped her shoulder against the door frame, but she didn't say anything in response to this provocation, and after a moment Joel muttered an apology.

'I just don't know what's wrong with him,' he sighed wearily. 'I mean, he's never been exactly happy living with

Louise and Stewart, but until recently he didn't have a lot of complaints. God knows, it's not what I want for him either, but I don't have an alternative.'

Olivia frowned. 'Why couldn't you and Louise share custody, at least until Sean's old enough to make an informed decision? Surely there's someone who could look after him when you're not here? Your mother, for instance.'

'Yeah, right.' Joel was sardonic. 'Like she's going to give up her freedom to look after a precocious ten-year-old.' He shook his head. 'And why should she? It's not her problem.'

'Sean's no one's problem,' said Olivia firmly. 'He's just a growing boy who wants to spend more time with his father. And—well, I think it might be a good idea to give him a break, if you can arrange it. If he's run away twice in one week, you have to see it as a cry for help.'

Joel's gaze sharpened. 'Has he told you something I should know?'

'No.' Olivia wrapped defensive arms about her midriff. 'It's just a feeling I have, that's all.' She paused. 'Couldn't he stay for a few days? Given enough time, he might tell you what's troubling him.'

Joel scowled. 'So you do think something's troubling him?'

Olivia sighed. 'At the risk of sounding like his social worker, I think he has—issues.'

'What issues?' Joel was perplexed.

'If I knew that, we wouldn't be having this conversation.' Olivia frowned. 'You know what it's like. When you're a child, problems assume a lot more importance than when you're older.' She paused. 'Can't you remember what you were like at his age?'

Joel looked up at her through lashes that were long and thick and dark as pitch. 'My memory doesn't kick in until the day you started at the comprehensive,' he told her roughly. 'You were waiting for the school bus when I got there and I thought—'

But he broke off at the point, pushing himself up and away from the unit, turning back to switch on the coffee machine. 'This won't take long,' he said, despising his sudden weakness. 'Then I'd better go and make my peace with Sean.'

'Would you like me to speak to him?' Olivia didn't know why she was prolonging this, but she knew it wasn't wholly for Sean's sake.

Joel shrugged, glancing at her over his shoulder. 'If you think you can talk some sense into him,' he said tersely, aware that Olivia gave him an impatient look before walking out of the room.

They were down again in a little over ten minutes. Sean still looked uneasy, but at least he wasn't sulking. 'Sorry, Dad,' he mumbled as they entered the kitchen, and then, with a quick look at Olivia, he came and gave Joel a hug.

Joel met Olivia's eyes over the boy's head, but he couldn't read anything from her expression. And, after returning the hug with interest, he turned his attention to the boy. 'That's OK, son,' he said, nodding towards the table. 'Sit down. I've made you a toasted cheese sandwich.'

'Cool,' said Sean at once, pulling out a chair and giving Olivia a grateful grin. It was obvious he was seeking her approval, and Joel wondered why it didn't annoy him that she seemed to have such a good rapport with his son.

'Coffee,' he offered, holding out a mug of the steaming beverage. Olivia took the cup and tasted it approvingly.

'Um, that's good,' she said, smiling at him now. 'You always made—that is, *I* always enjoy a good cup of coffee.'

She'd almost betrayed their previous relationship, she realised, wondering if Joel was aware of it. It wasn't that she wanted to hide it from Sean, but right now she felt he had enough to contend with.

'Let's go into the sitting room,' Joel said now. He smiled at his son. 'Finish your sandwich first, right?'

'OK, Dad.'

Sean seemed quite content to do as he was told for the moment, but Joel guessed that as soon as his stomach was full he'd begin to have second thoughts.

Which was why he wanted to have a quick word with Olivia before his son joined them. But to his surprise, she apologised as soon as they were out of earshot of Sean. 'I'm sorry,' she said. 'I mean, I don't mind if you tell him.' She paused. 'But perhaps he doesn't need to hear it right this minute.'

Joel's brows drew together. 'Am I missing something here? What doesn't he need to hear right this minute?'

'That we were married,' she said awkwardly, aware that their time alone was limited. Then, when he continued to regard her uncomprehendingly, 'Well, obviously you didn't notice the slip I almost made. I'm sorry I mentioned it.'

She subsided huffily onto a soft leather sofa, one of two that flanked an open grate set in a delicate marble surround. Taking another sip of coffee, she cradled the mug between her palms, feeling frustrated. Was she the only one who was aware of the anomalies here? He was asking his first wife for advice about the child he'd had with his second, and she was worrying because she'd almost said the wrong thing. Unbelievable!

To her surprise—and a certain amount of apprehension—Joel came and sat beside her. The powerful muscles of his thigh depressed the cushion nearest to her. And, when he leaned forward to set his coffee mug on a glass-topped occasional table in front of the sofa, the hem of his shirt separated from his trousers.

Dear lord!

She sat back abruptly, directing her eyes anywhere but at that tantalising wedge of brown skin. Yet, she couldn't deny, there was something incredibly vulnerable about it. It proved how agitated he'd been when he'd got into his car at the university. He hadn't even stopped to grab a jacket before making the twelve-mile drive to Millford.

Her eyes darted irresistibly in his direction again. Evidently, he still tanned as easily as he had used to when they were together. An image of them skinny-dipping in Redes Bay when they were teenagers was as vivid now as it was unwelcome.

But he ensured she couldn't ignore him for long, whatever her feelings. Turning towards her, he unsettled her still more by laying one arm along the back of the sofa behind her. 'Now, tell me what you mean,' he said as her eyes fastened on the cluster of hairs just visible in the open V of his shirt. 'Don't you want Sean to know about us?'

'There is no "us",' she told him stiffly, in no state to have this conversation.

'I know that.' His voice rasped. 'But there used to be.'

Now, why had he said that? Joel asked himself irritably.

Just because he was sitting so close to her, because he could smell the indefinable perfume of her skin, he'd spoken recklessly. But it wouldn't do. Dammit, she'd always been able to drive him crazy when he was near her. Right now, all his heat-hazed brain could think about was that scene in his office and how much he wanted to touch her again.

But it wasn't going to happen!

Then she spoke, her voice low and a little unsteady, and the intimacy of their situation swept over him again. 'It's up to you—whether you want to tell him or not. I just didn't want to say the wrong thing.'

'As opposed to doing the wrong thing,' he muttered, unable to pull his eyes away from the rounded swell of her breasts. She was wearing a black T-shirt today and tight jeans that emphasised the slender curves below her waist. And a scarlet chiffon scarf, like a flag of defiance. He would have liked to wind that scarf around his hand and use it to drag her provocative body into his arms. 'Yeah, I see what you mean.'

'Are you saying I've done the wrong thing by coming here?' she asked, her words distracting him, and Joel closed his eyes for a moment against the pull of an attraction he'd been sure he'd conquered long ago.

'No, I have,' he said at last, opening his eyes again and scowling at her. 'By inviting you into my house.'

Her lips parted. 'Well, I'm sorry—' she began indignantly, but he didn't let her finish. Before he could control the impulse, he'd reached out and brushed his knuckles over the visible peaks of her breasts. He was almost sure she wasn't wearing a bra, and the notion drove all sane thoughts out of his head.

'Joel!'

She scrambled backwards, but he was too quick for her, his hand reaching for the arm of the sofa, keeping her in her seat. 'Now do you see what I mean?' he demanded, gazing down at her with oddly possessive eyes. He used his free hand to trace a tantalising path from her breast to the button at her waist. 'I'm wondering if we had sex together if it might help me to get you out of my skull. What do you think?'

'In your dreams!' Olivia sucked in a trembling breath, horrified by her own reaction to his outrageous suggestion. Oh, yeah, her libido applauded. Go for it, girl! Let's get it on. But what she forced herself to say was, 'Let me get up, Joel. I'll get out of here and solve your problem.'

Joel shook his head. 'You think it's that easy?'

Olivia didn't think it was easy at all. Her heart was pounding, her pulse was erratic, and her body felt as if it was on fire. If she wasn't careful, he was going to realise her dilemma, and that made her edgy. 'I have no desire to have sex with you, Joel,' she insisted, and then recoiled with a gasp when his nail scraped down her zip.

For a breath-stealing moment she thought he'd opened it, and she knew her panties were already wet. Heavens, she thought with relief, discovering she'd been mistaken, if he'd slipped his hand inside her jeans he'd have soon found out what a liar she was.

But he wasn't finished with her. 'Sure?' he asked, lowering himself until his chest was just touching hers. The clean male smell she'd noticed earlier rose from his opened shirt, and she could tell from the stubble on his jawline that he hadn't shaved since the night before.

She couldn't deny the moan that rose into her throat as he deliberately pressed closer. His chin scraped her cheek and he used both hands to pull her T-shirt out of her jeans. Then warm palms spread against her midriff, his thumbs brushing the undersides of her breasts with wilful intent.

'In my dreams, hmm?' he taunted her softly, and this time she wasn't mistaken about the invasion of his hand. 'Oh, baby,' he muttered thickly as his fingers found her secret, and then his mouth sought hers and the room began to spin dizzily about her.

The sound of footsteps crossing the parquet floor was instantly sobering. 'Damn,' muttered Joel savagely, hauling himself away from her, and by the time the boy appeared in the doorway his father was standing by the window, apparently watching the lambs in the distant field.

Olivia didn't want to get up. Her legs felt like jelly and every nerve in her body felt as raw as an open wound. But she had to prove—to herself as well as Joel—that she was no pushover. Pushing her T-shirt down and herself up, she turned to smile at the boy.

'Feeling better?' she asked with assumed brightness and Sean made a face.

'That depends,' he muttered, his eyes moving to his father. 'What have you two been talking about?'

'Not that it's any business of yours,' said Joel irritably, and Sean hung his head.

But the truth was, Joel was feeling both thwarted and guilty. Dammit, his son was more important than the unwanted hunger Olivia inspired in him. Yet he only had to look at her to feel again the mindless need of total fascination.

How many more times was he going to let her make a fool of him? OK, she hadn't exactly invited him to make love to her, but she hadn't tried very hard to stop him either. Aching with frustration, he struggled to remember what was important here.

'I'll—talk to your mother,' he told the boy flatly, and then wished he hadn't made it sound like a done deal when Sean flung himself into his arms.

'Thanks, Dad!' he exclaimed fervently. 'I knew Olivia would help you see it my way.'

'Olivia?'

Joel scowled, and Olivia hastily tried to put him straight. 'I just said I was sure you'd put things right with his mother,' she mumbled awkwardly, and Joel gave her a suspicious look.

But when he spoke to his son, he didn't question it. 'I'm not promising anything, Sean,' he said, peeling the boy's arms from around him and holding him by his shoulders. 'But I've got to tell her where you are, anyway, and I'm sure she'll agree to let you spend the night here at least.'

She'd better, Joel added silently, meeting Olivia's eyes again, letting her see his frustration. When would Louise have asked him about their son's whereabouts? he wondered angrily. Did she even care?

Then, realising Olivia would interpret his expression differently, he continued, 'You approve?'

Olivia lifted her shoulders but, before she could make any response, Sean intervened. 'Just tonight?' he asked plaintively, and she realised he did tend to push his luck with his father.

'Look, I've got to be going,' she said, hoping to prevent another confrontation. 'Nice to meet you, Sean.'

Sean's face dropped, and he swung away from Joel to stare at her. 'But we'll see you again, won't we?' he protested. And then, to his father, 'Olivia's staying with her father, too,' almost as if their situations were comparable.

'I know.' Joel nodded. 'Say goodbye, Sean. And thank Mrs—'

'Olivia,' put in his son at once. 'She said I could call her Olivia.'

'OK.' Joel forced a tight smile. 'Thank—her for taking the trouble to bring you here.' Then, gritting his teeth, 'We both appreciate it.'

'Do you?'

Olivia's lips twisted and Joel's stomach tightened in spite of all his efforts to ignore what had happened. Dammit, was having an affair with her the only way he was going to get her out of his mind?

'You better believe it,' he responded now, but even to his own ears he sounded rattled. 'Sean?'

'Oh, yeah. Thanks, Olivia.' His son had no such hang-ups. 'But I can come and see you at the farm, can't I?'

'Sean!'

'Of course you can,' she responded, her eyes challenging Joel to contradict her. 'See you—both—later.'

CHAPTER EIGHT

OLIVIA drove back to Bridgeford, her head buzzing. What had happened to all her brave predictions of not getting involved with her ex-husband? Here she was, befriending his son, letting Joel back into her life and her emotions.

And why?

In Sean's case, it was easy. She liked him, she liked him a lot. All her thwarted maternal instincts came to the fore when she saw how unhappy he was.

With Joel, however, it was anything but easy to understand. Hadn't he hurt her enough? Was she so desperate for a man that she was prepared to go to any lengths to satisfy her sexual needs? If so, she was pathetic!

But that wasn't the whole story. In truth, she'd forgotten how vulnerable she'd always been where Joel was concerned. Hadn't that day at his office taught her anything? She should have remembered that in the old days he'd only had to look at her in a certain way and she'd be begging him to make love to her.

She'd only been fourteen when she'd become aware that Joel was interested in her. Oh, she'd noticed how attractive he was. All her friends had thought he was totally hot! Ironic, really, that Jayne had used the same adjective. But it had been such a thrill when he'd first asked her out.

Naturally, her sister had warned her against getting involved with a boy who was older than she was. At fourteen, sixteen had seemed like a great age. But she hadn't been willing to listen to anyone's advice. She'd assured Linda she knew what she was doing. The physical attraction that had initially brought them together had deepened into love, and she'd believed that nothing and no one would ever split her and Joel up.

Until she'd succeeded in doing it herself...

Martin's car was in the yard when she got back to the farm, and she took a guilty glance at her watch. It was a quarter-past eleven, three-quarters of an hour later than she'd intended. But surely, when she explained the circumstances, they'd understand.

However, when she entered the kitchen, only Linda was sitting at the table, glancing through some coloured brochures spread out in front of her.

'Hi,' said Olivia awkwardly. 'Sorry I'm late.'

Linda looked up. 'Where have you been?'

'To Millford.' Olivia realised some further explanation was needed, and added, 'Joel's son needed a lift.'

'Joel's son?' Linda frowned. 'You mean Sean?'

'Mmm.' Olivia moved to the stove to help herself to some coffee, not wanting Linda to study her too closely. 'Where's Martin?'

'He's gone to help Andy clear out one of the cottages.' Linda got up from her chair. 'How did you meet Sean Armstrong? I didn't know you knew him. Shouldn't he have been in school?'

'I expect so.' Olivia looked down into her cup of coffee, refusing to meet her sister's accusing gaze. She told herself she wouldn't be intimidated into revealing things that were really none of Linda's business. 'What did you want to talk to me about?'

Linda was taken aback. 'Oh, well, Martin's not here at the moment—'

'I'm sure you don't need Martin to hold your hand,' said Olivia, her taste buds protesting at the bitter taste of the coffee. 'Come on, Linda. Do you want me to leave?'

'Heavens, no!' Linda sounded horrified. 'You're welcome to stay here as long as you like.'

'So?'

Linda sighed, and then she bent and picked up one of the brochures she'd been looking at when Olivia came in and handed it over. 'What do you think of that?'

Olivia put down her coffee and looked at the glossy publication. It had been issued by the local tourist board and contained a list of holiday accommodation in the area. It dealt primarily with farms offering bed and breakfast and others that had cottages to rent.

'Well?' There was a trace of excitement in Linda's voice now. 'Could Martin and I handle something like that?'

Olivia blinked. 'Offer bed and breakfast, you mean?'

'No!' Linda clicked her tongue. 'We don't have enough room here to offer bed and breakfast. No, I meant the cottages. We want to modernise the ones we have and offer them as holiday rentals. What do you think?'

Olivia looked at the brochure again, trying to concentrate. 'But aren't the cottages occupied?'

'Not any more,' said Linda at once. 'I told you about the

sheep and cattle being destroyed. There was no point in paying men we didn't need and couldn't afford.'

'You asked them to leave?'

Linda was dismissive. 'Some of them left of their own accord. They got jobs elsewhere.'

'And the rest?'

'I believe they were offered council accommodation.' She sighed. 'It wasn't our problem. Livvy. We all have to do what's necessary to make a living.'

Olivia shook her head. She doubted she could have been so ruthless. Or her father either. Had this had anything to do with his illness? It must have been a blow when he lost everything.

Now she said, 'If you think renovating the cottages is viable, go for it.' She hesitated. 'What does Dad say?'

'Oh, you know Dad.' Linda was impatient. 'In any case, he's not running the farm now, Martin is. And once Dad sees how successful we are, he'll come round. It's not as if he's ever going to be able to run the place himself again.'

Olivia shrugged. 'Well, it's really nothing to do with me, is it? I mean, I don't live here.'

Linda bit her lip. 'No,' she conceded. 'But—well, we do need your help.'

'My help?'

'Yes.' Linda hesitated. 'Look, I won't beat about the bush, we need—financial assistance. We can't go to the bank because they won't lend Martin any money while the farm still belongs to Dad. And you know what he's like about going into debt.'

Olivia stared at her. 'So Dad's opposed to this venture, then?'

'Need you ask? He's never forgiven us for giving the men notice. He's not practical, Livvy. Whatever he thinks, we can't live on fresh air.'

Olivia nodded. Actually, she sympathised with their predicament. She might not like Martin, but she'd never accuse him of being lazy. And the leisure industry was booming.

'It sounds—feasible,' she said at last. 'I'm sure you'll have no trouble attracting visitors to this area. But—' She pulled a face. 'I can't help you, Linda. I wish I could, but I don't have any money. Just enough for a deposit on an apartment, if I'm lucky.'

Linda looked stunned. 'You're not serious.'

'I'm afraid I am.'

'But you told Dad that Bruce was a wealthy man.'

'He was.' And then before Linda could interrupt her again, she went on, 'I left Bruce, Linda. He didn't want me to and consequently there was no generous settlement when we divorced. Besides, I didn't want any of his money. I wanted a clean break. That's partly why I came back to England.'

'But what about your own money? You'd been earning a good salary. What happened to that?'

Olivia was tempted to say it was none of her sister's business, but she didn't want to fall out with her, so she answered truthfully, 'Lawyers' fees are expensive, Linda. And although I earned a healthy salary when I was in London, I'm afraid I never saw the need to save in those days.'

'So why did you leave Bruce? Was there someone else?'

'Not as far as I was concerned, no.'

'But if you're saying he was the guilty party,' Linda said, 'you were entitled to half his assets, weren't you?'

Olivia didn't want to get into the reasons for the break-up or relate how impossible it would have been for her to prove that Bruce was seeing someone else. 'I just wanted out of the relationship,' she said quietly. 'I'm sorry, Linda. I wish I could help you, but I can't.'

'Yes, well, being sorry isn't going to pay for the renovations. Those cottages have needed updating for years.'

Olivia sat down in the chair opposite. 'If there was anything I could do—'

'There is.' As if the idea had just occurred to her, Linda stared at her through narrowed eyes. 'You could talk to Dad, persuade him that this is the only way to keep the farm.'

'Oh, I don't know…'

'Why not? You said you wanted to help, and he'll listen to you. You're the prodigal daughter. If you say you're in favour, he might be prepared to consider getting a loan.'

As luck would have it, Andy came in at that moment and Olivia was able to make her escape without answering her. She knew it was only a temporary release, that sooner or later she would have to come to a decision. But for now, she was grateful for the chance to be on her own.

But, in the days that followed, it seemed that Martin had persuaded his wife to give her sister some breathing space. The plan wasn't mentioned again and Olivia was able to pretend she didn't have the sword of Damocles hanging over her head. Instead she pursued her efforts to get her father to use a wheelchair, seducing him with promises of taking him out in her car, away from the prying eyes of Bridgeford.

Nurse Franklin agreed with her and, whether she thought that leaving them alone together would achieve her own ends or not, Linda put her considerable weight behind it, too. So much so that Ben Foley said he was heartily weary of being put upon. But then he delighted them all by agreeing to give the wheelchair a chance.

Consequently, a week later, Olivia and Linda helped the old man out of the wheelchair and into the front seat of the Renault. It had been arranged that Olivia would drive him down to the coast and Linda had prepared a flask of coffee for them to take with them. She was evidently doing her best to sweeten the atmosphere and Olivia had been so pleased with her father's progress that she hadn't thought of leaving for days.

Olivia drove to Redes Bay, driving down the precarious cliff road and parking on the dunes above the beach. The place seemed deserted; the children were all in school and it was too early in the season for holidaymakers to brave the cool north-east wind that was blowing off the sea. Across the road from the beach, the small pub was doing better business, but no one was taking advantage of the outdoor tables today.

However, inside the car it was snug and cosy. And the view was magnificent: a stretch of almost deserted sand with the white-capped waves stretching as far as the eye could see. Ben Foley heaved a sigh and then turned his head to look at his daughter. 'Thanks for this,' he said sheepishly. 'I've been an old fool, haven't I?'

'Just stubborn,' said Olivia gently. 'No change there, then. Now, do you want a cup of Linda's coffee? Or would you rather have a beer?'

Her father gaped. 'A beer,' he said fervently. 'It's six months since I had a beer.'

'You're probably not supposed to have alcohol,' said

Olivia doubtfully, half wishing she hadn't mentioned it. 'But one beer won't do any harm, will it?'

Her father agreed, and, leaving him sitting in the car, she walked across the road to the pub. She was wearing jeans and a warm woollen jersey but she was still cold. She really would have to toughen up, she thought, if she was going to make her home in this area.

Now, where had that come from?

She'd been thinking about it for some time, she realised. Having got to know her father again, she was loath to go back to London and only get the chance to see him a couple of times a year. If she got a job with an estate agency in Newcastle, she could buy herself an apartment there. That way, she'd be able to visit the farm as often as she could.

There was a big four-wheel-drive vehicle parked in front of the pub. It looked like Joel's Lexus, she thought uneasily, but when she stepped into the bar there was no sign of him. And, after all, she told herself as she ordered her father a beer and herself a diet cola, there must be other cars like his in the area. When the weather was bad, a four-wheel-drive vehicle was invaluable.

After paying for the drinks she stepped outside again, shivering as a gust of wind blew her hair across her face. Scooping it back, she hurried across the road to where she'd left the Renault, and then stopped short when she saw the man beside her car.

It was Joel.

So what's new? she thought irritably. Although it was over a week since she'd seen him, she couldn't deny she'd thought about him. A lot. And Sean, she defended herself, noticing that her father didn't seem to have any objections to the visitor. His door was open and Joel was standing with one arm draped across the roof of the vehicle and one foot propped on the sill.

Joel straightened at her approach, though she observed the smile he'd been giving her father was distinctly thinner when it was directed at her. In tight jeans and a black T-shirt, a leather jacket left open, he didn't seem to feel the cold. 'Liv,' he said, and she didn't know whether to get into the car or stand and face him. 'Linda said I'd find you here.'

Olivia frowned. 'You went to the farm?'

'No.' Joel spoke levelly. 'I tried your mobile—'

'How did you know my number?'

Olivia spoke impulsively, but Joel merely said, 'My phone records all calls.' He paused. 'Anyway, as you probably know, I could only get voicemail. That was when I called the farm.'

'Oh.' Olivia remembered rather guiltily that she'd turned her phone off. But she'd reasoned that no one was likely to call her here. 'So you spoke to Linda?'

'Right.' Joel was patient. 'She said you'd taken your father to the coast, so I guessed you'd come here.'

'Did you?' Olivia's lips twisted.

'Yes.' His grey eyes were penetrating. 'I knew it was a favourite haunt of yours.'

'Of yours, too, if I remember correctly,' she replied tartly. Then, as his eyes darkened, 'Why did you want to speak to me?'

Joel sighed. 'I've got a problem.'

'What kind of a problem?'

'Why don't the two of you go for a walk along the beach and he can tell you?' suggested her father, mopping

his mouth. 'I'll just sit here and enjoy my beer in peace.'
He held out his good hand. 'Joel, will you just unscrew the
cap for me?'

Olivia was forced to hand the bottle to Joel and she
watched somewhat resentfully as he opened it and put it
into Ben Foley's hand. There was a gentleness about him
as he dealt with her father that she hated to acknowledge.
But it was there just the same: an understanding of the old
man's dignity that she couldn't ignore.

'I don't have a coat,' she said now, wrapping her arms
about herself.

'Here, you wear this,' said Joel, taking off his leather
jacket. 'I've got a duffel in the boot.'

'No, it's all right,' she began, but he'd already shed the
coat and wrapped its folds around her.

'Just give me a second,' he said, and sprinted off across
the road to where the Lexus was parked.

'I didn't say the wrong thing, did I?' her father asked
anxiously and Olivia was obliged to reassure him.

'No—'

'I mean, he picked you up from the airport, didn't he?
And Linda tells me you gave his son a lift to Millford the
other day.'

'It's OK, Dad.' Olivia forced a smile. 'Now, are you sure
you'll be all right on your own?'

'I'm not a baby, Liv,' he said, the unparalysed side of
his face twisting in resignation. 'Besides, it'll be good for
the two of you to catch up.'

To catch up!

Olivia gritted her teeth and thrust her arms into the
sleeves of the soft leather jacket. As if she and Joel needed

to catch up. It would be truer to say they knew too much about one another as it was.

Even so, she couldn't deny the jacket protected her from the wind. It was redolent with his distinctive maleness, still warm from the heat of his body, and she wrapped it closely about her. And refused to accept that her rising temperature was caused by anything more than the quality of the leather.

Joel came loping back wearing a hooded duffel. Once again the coat was unfastened, but his hands in the pockets kept the two sides together. 'All set?' he asked, with a quick smile for her father.

'As I'll ever be,' said Olivia ungraciously, but he had to understand this was at his instigation not hers. She'd half expected him to avoid the farm so long as she was around.

They left the car and walked down the path that led through the dunes and onto the beach. The wind was considerably stronger here, and Olivia sucked in a breath as it tried to drag the jacket sides away. 'Let me,' said Joel, and, brushing her hands away, he swiftly attached the zip and pulled it up to her chin. 'Now put your hands in the pockets,' he instructed. 'That should work.'

Olivia did as he said because her fingers were already tingling with the cold. And it was true, now that the jacket was fastened, it had no chance to billow in the wind.

'Thanks,' she said offhandedly, and Joel cast her an ironic look.

'Yeah, right,' he said, and then cursed as the soft sand spilled into his loafers. Emptying them out, he walked barefoot onto the firmer sand.

Admiring his fortitude, Olivia hurried after him, grateful

that her own boots prevented the sand from invading her feet. Not that Joel appeared to notice that the firmer sand was damp and chilly. With his gaze fixed on the horizon, he seemed indifferent to his surroundings. And to her.

'You wanted to talk to me?' she prompted, not happy at being ignored when he'd come here expressly to find her. She glanced up at his unsmiling face. 'How's Sean?'

Joel's jaw compressed. 'Do you care?'

Olivia caught her breath. 'You know I do.'

'Do I?'

Olivia sighed. 'Is this going to be another pointless argument? Of course I care about Sean.' She paused, her eyes widening. 'Don't tell me he's run away again.'

'No.' Joel blew out a breath. 'As a matter of fact, Louise and I have come to an agreement. She's letting Sean stay with me for the next two weeks.'

'That's great!'

Olivia was genuinely pleased for him, but Joel's expression didn't change. 'It's not great as it goes,' he told her flatly. 'I told her I'd be available, but now I won't.'

Olivia frowned. 'Why not?'

'Because the tutor who was going to cover my absence has broken his hip.' Joel grimaced. 'Hell, I feel sorry for the guy, but it couldn't have happened at a worse time as far as I'm concerned.'

Olivia's brows ascended. 'So—what now?'

Joel bent his head, aware that when she'd left his house in Millford a week ago he'd determined that, whatever Sean said, they weren't going to be seeing Olivia again. Yet here he was, telling her his troubles, hoping, he acknowledged ruefully, that she'd be able to help him out. Again.

'When are you leaving?' he asked suddenly, and Olivia pulled a hand out of the pocket of the jacket and pressed it to her throat.

'Well, that's pointed enough,' she remarked, despising herself for feeling hurt by it. 'What's it to you? You're not going to tell me you'll miss me. That would be totally out of character.'

'Can't you stop trying to score points, Liv?' Joel sounded weary. 'I only asked when you were leaving because I was hoping you might be agreeable to working for me for a couple of weeks.'

'Working for you?' Olivia stared at him. Then comprehension dawned. 'You want me to look after Sean?'

'Yeah.' Joel bent and picked up a pebble and sent it skittering across the waves. 'I know it's presumptuous and you're probably going to blow me out, but I do think you're the only person I could ask.'

Olivia shook her head. 'And what would I have to do?'

'Not a lot.' Joel looked at her. 'Just take him to school in the mornings and pick him up again at half-past three. Then stay with him until I get home. He can wait and have his supper with me. I can't give you my actual schedule. It can change from day to day. But unless I have any evening tutorials, most days I'm home about six.'

Olivia's breathing quickened. 'And while Sean's at school?'

'Your time's your own, of course.'

'I'd sleep at the farm.'

Joel looked away. 'Of course.'

Olivia considered. 'Well—OK. I'll do it.' She paused. 'But I don't need any payment. I'll do it for Sean.'

Joel exhaled heavily. 'I don't need charity, Liv.'

'Nor do I,' Olivia retorted shortly. She glanced back along the beach to where she'd left the car. 'If that's settled, I presume we can go back.'

CHAPTER NINE

On Monday morning Olivia was up at half-past six.

Hurrying into the bathroom, she washed her face and cleaned her teeth, and then, because it felt chilly, she dressed in warm woollen trousers and a purple sweater. She didn't bother with much make-up, just a trace of eyeliner, mascara and a smear of lip gloss. Then, with her leather coat over her arm, she went downstairs.

Linda wasn't about, but someone—Martin, possibly—had made a pot of tea and left toast crumbs all over the drainer. Olivia wasn't hungry, but she poured herself a cup of lukewarm tea and drank it on the move.

She still had to tell the rest of the family what she was doing, and as she swept the crumbs away and washed both her cup and Martin's she hoped they would approve.

Her father knew, naturally. She hadn't been able to hide what Joel had wanted from him, and he'd looked at her a little oddly when he heard that she and Joel were planning to share responsibility for the boy.

'Are you sure about this, Liv?' he'd asked as they drove back to the farm. 'I mean, giving the kid a lift is one thing. Committing yourself to two weeks of driving back and forth to Millford, just so Sean can spend a few days with his father, does seem quite a chore.'

'You can't say two weeks on the one hand and then imply it's only for a few days on the other,' Olivia had pointed out evenly. And then, because she'd known her father was only thinking of her, 'Well—I couldn't refuse, could I?'

'Why not?' Ben Foley had been indignant. 'OK, you and Joel have got history. No one can deny that. But he got over you soon enough and married the Webster girl. What does she think about you looking after her son?'

'I doubt if she knows.' Olivia had been terse, stung by her father's assessment of Joel's behaviour. Was that what he'd done? she'd wondered. It had been galling to think that that was what everyone in Bridgeford thought.

Thankfully, the old man hadn't questioned how well she knew Sean. He'd probably assumed the boy had accompanied Joel when he'd picked her up at the airport. But Linda had still to be told and she could only hope it wouldn't become a bone of contention, before she told her what she was doing.

Joel had said Sean had to leave for school at a quarter-past eight, but Olivia realised it was only a quarter-to when she reached Millford. She was far too early and, not wanting to look too eager, she parked some distance from the house and got out of the car.

Millford was smaller than Bridgeford, but just as picturesque. Pulling her coat out of the back of the car, she put it on and strolled across to the church.

Evidently there'd been an early-morning service and the vicar was standing at the door, saying goodbye to the few stalwarts who'd braved the uncertain weather. Olivia halted by the lych-gate, feeling an odd sense of familiarity when she looked at the man. But that was silly, she thought impatiently. She'd never been to this church before.

She was about to turn away when he hailed her. 'Liv! Olivia,' he called, striding towards her. 'My goodness, it is you. What are you doing in Millford?'

Olivia watched the man as he approached, realising why he'd seemed so familiar. Despite the fact that his angular frame was disguised by the flapping folds of his surplice and he'd lost most of his hair, she recognised him at once.

'Brian!' she exclaimed. 'My Go—I mean, Brian Webster!' She paused. 'You're a vicar!'

'For my sins,' he said drily. 'And Olivia Foley.' He said her name again. 'I heard you were in the States.'

'I was.' Olivia shook her head. 'And I thought you were in the army.'

'For almost eight years.' He nodded. 'I thought it was what I wanted to do, but after Kosovo—' He blew out a harsh breath. 'I knew I had to get out.'

'But a vicar!' Olivia could see that he was still emotionally disturbed by his memories and tried to lighten the mood. 'Who'd have thought it? Brian Webster! Mrs Sawyer's personal nemesis. I don't think she ever got over you putting that frog in her desk.'

Brian laughed. 'Innocent times,' he said ruefully. 'Today it would probably be a tarantula or something equally terrifying.'

Olivia smiled. 'So how long have you been—living here?'

'How long have I been a vicar, do you mean?' He turned briefly to acknowledge one of his parishioners. 'About five years, give or take. How about you? Are you staying with your dad?'

'At present,' said Olivia, remembering that time was passing and she really ought to go. But with that thought came another: Brian Webster was Louise's cousin. If Joel hadn't informed his ex-wife of the arrangements he'd made, she was soon going to find out.

'So what are you doing in Millford?' Brian frowned, detecting she was uncomfortable with that question. 'Don't tell me you're looking for Joel Armstrong! I thought that was all over between you two long ago.'

'It was. It *is*.' Olivia glanced away across the green to where Joel's house was situated. 'I—well, his son's staying with him at the moment and I've promised to give Sean a lift to school.'

Brian regarded her curiously. 'You?' he said blankly. 'Why can't Joel take him himself?'

'Because I said I'd do it,' replied Olivia, not wanting to discuss Joel's schedule or her own. 'And I'd better get going. They're expecting me.'

Brian stepped back, spreading his arms dramatically. 'Well, don't let me hold you up,' he said, though she sensed he didn't approve. 'Perhaps I'll see you again—when you're visiting Millford,' he added pointedly. 'Give Joel my best, won't you? Tell him it's too long since he graced the doors of my church.'

'I will.'

Olivia smiled as she turned away, but she doubted Joel would appreciate the sentiment. He and Brian had never liked one another, due in no small part to the fact that Brian had been in her year at school. They had just been friends, but Brian had loved to rub Joel's nose in it, exaggerating their closeness and chiding him about babysnatching when Olivia and Joel got together.

She was tempted to leave the car where it was, but that would have looked foolish, so she slipped behind the wheel and drove the few yards to Joel's house. However, as she shifted into neutral, Joel came out of the door and down the path, and she knew at once that he'd seen her talking to the other man.

'At last,' he said harshly, pulling her door open. 'I was beginning to wonder if you'd forgotten why you were here.'

'And good morning to you, too,' retorted Olivia, swinging her legs out of the car and getting to her feet. 'It's only five-past eight, Joel. I've got plenty of time.'

She met his brooding gaze with a defiance she was far from feeling, but for once Joel was the first to look away. 'OK,' he said. 'Perhaps that was unjustified. But before I go, I want to give you some—some information.'

'Don't you mean instructions?' Olivia taunted. 'Come on, Joel. I have looked after kids before. One of Bruce's business colleagues had twins and they didn't come to any harm when their parents left them with me.'

Joel sighed, allowing her to precede him into the house. 'If I've offended you, I'm sorry,' he said heavily, and she actually thought he meant it. 'But this situation is new to me, and I don't want anything to go wrong.'

'Like Louise finding out?' suggested Olivia, waiting for him to close the door and then following him across the hall and into the kitchen. 'Well, I'm sorry about that, but you should have warned me that Brian Webster was the vicar of All Saints Church.'

Joel grimaced. 'The vicar of All Saints,' he echoed. 'Why does that make me want to laugh?'

'You did see us, then?'

'Oh, yeah.' Joel heaved a sigh. 'I wasn't spying on you,' he added. 'I was in Sean's bedroom, trying to persuade him to get dressed, and I happened to look out of the window.' He shook his head. 'Brian Webster, preaching the good word to the people. After the things he said to me when you and I split up.'

Olivia wanted to ask him what Brian had said, but something else Joel had mentioned was more important. 'You were trying to persuade Sean to get dressed?' she asked, confused. 'Don't he and I have to leave in about ten minutes?'

'You do.' Joel was resigned. 'Oh, don't worry, he's had his breakfast. But he's decided that, as you're coming, he doesn't want to go to school.'

Olivia stared at him. 'But doesn't he know I'll be picking him up from school this afternoon?'

'Well, that won't be necessary today, actually,' said Joel apologetically. 'I'm free from two-thirty, so I can pick him up myself.'

Ridiculously, Olivia was disappointed. But what had she expected? That Joel would want her in his house any more often than was absolutely necessary? 'I see,' she said, trying not to let her feelings show. 'Well, you've got my number if you need it.'

'Yeah, right.'

Joel regarded her through narrowed eyes for a moment and now she was forced to look away. 'Was that all you wanted to tell me?' she asked, much too aware of how easily he could get under her skin. 'As you're picking him up—'

'These are for you,' Joel interrupted her, holding out a bunch of keys. 'You might as well have them. You'll need them tomorrow afternoon, anyway.'

Olivia's lips parted. 'These are for the house?'

'What else?'

'But—are you sure you want me to have them?' She moistened her lips nervously. 'I mean, you said—'

'I know what I said,' Joel told her harshly, not at all sure he was doing the right thing. But it was too late now. 'The situation's changed,' he added. 'And I won't be here when you are, will I?'

'Won't you?'

Not if I have any sense, thought Joel grimly, but he said, 'I'll go and give Sean a shout.'

However, before he reached the door, they both heard the boy's feet running down the stairs. Sean paused in the doorway, gazing at both of them with anxious eyes. 'I've changed my mind,' he said unnecessarily, though his shirt was buttoned unevenly and his tie was skewed. 'You're not sending Olivia away, are you?'

'Why would I do that?' Joel was impatient. What did Olivia have that caused both him and his son to make fools of themselves over her? 'Come here, kid. Let me put that tie straight.'

Sean beamed at Olivia as he did so. 'You're taking me to school,' he said, and she nodded. 'Cool!'

When Olivia got back to the farm, Martin and Andy were sitting at the kitchen table, tucking into bacon, eggs and sausages. She knew they sometimes came back for a proper breakfast, so she wasn't surprised. But when Linda turned from the stove, there was something less pleasant about her expression.

'Where've you been?' she asked, and, although Olivia resented her tone, she had the feeling her sister already knew.

'Um—Sean's staying with Joel at the moment and he needed someone to take him to school, so I—'

'Volunteered,' broke in Linda scornfully. 'Honestly, Livvy, I'd have thought you had more sense.'

'I didn't volunteer.' Olivia flushed in spite of herself. 'Joel asked me to do it. Didn't Dad explain?'

'Dad?' Her sister looked puzzled. 'Dad knew?'

Now Olivia looked doubtful. 'Well, yes, I thought—oh, was it Brian Webster?'

'Louise rang,' said Linda, scowling. 'One of the other mothers saw you delivering Sean to school and called her. She wants to speak to you about it. I told her I'd get you to give her a ring as soon as you got back.'

'Did you?' Olivia objected to Linda making any promises on her behalf. 'Well, don't worry. I'll go and see her. I want to know what kind of mother doesn't know— or care—if her son's missing.'

Linda blinked. 'Sean's not missing.'

'He was.' Immediately regretting the impulse to put Linda on the defensive, Olivia was forced to explain how she'd found Sean in the barn. 'And it wasn't the first time,' she declared defiantly. 'He doesn't want to live with his mother. He wants to live with Joel.'

Linda grimaced. 'I see.' She paused. 'And I suppose Joel can't look after the kid on his own.'

'No.'

'He could employ someone,' Linda said thoughtfully. 'Other people do.'

'Perhaps you should offer to look after the boy on a permanent basis,' suggested Martin surprisingly. 'I'm sure he'd be willing to pay you the going rate.'

'Oh, I don't think so…'

Olivia shook her head, but she had to admit it wasn't totally off the wall. After all, Joel had offered to pay her. But she was a trained estate agent, not a nanny.

'You should give it some thought,' Linda put in, after exchanging a glance with her husband. 'That way you wouldn't have to leave Bridgeford. I know you're worried about Dad and you'd like to stick around.'

Olivia was taken aback. 'Well, I had thought of getting a job in Newcastle,' she confessed, and Linda nodded eagerly.

'That's a great idea,' she agreed. 'Then you wouldn't need to buy an apartment. You could stay here with us.'

Olivia was getting the sense that she was missing something here. 'But—wouldn't that be an imposition?' she asked warily.

'Heck, no.' It was Martin who spoke now, wiping his mouth with the back of his hand. 'This is as much your home as ours. If you can put up with us.'

Olivia didn't know what to say. 'Well—thanks,' she said at last. 'I do appreciate it. But if I get a job in Newcastle, I'll buy an apartment there.' She took a breath. 'I'm sure you'll agree that one bathroom isn't enough for five of you, let alone six.'

'Dad can't get upstairs,' pointed out Linda at once.

'And we're thinking of dividing the main bedroom so

Linda and I can have an *en suite* shower room,' Martin added swiftly. 'Anyway, at least think about it, Livvy. We are your family. And I know Ben would be delighted if you stayed.'

Which was probably true, Olivia conceded, accepting a cup of tea from Linda but refusing anything else. She felt a little hollow inside, but she wasn't hungry. All of a sudden she had a family again, and she wished she didn't feel as if none of them was being quite sincere.

Church Close was, as Sean had said, a road of new mock-Tudor houses. Driving into the road later that morning, Olivia hoped she was doing the right thing. She had no idea if Joel would approve of what she was going to say to Louise really. But she had to put the woman straight about hers and Joel's relationship. The last thing she needed was more gossip about her and her ex-husband.

Belatedly, it occurred to her that Louise might not be at home now. Sean had said his mother had a job, and it was certainly true that most of the houses in the road looked unoccupied. There was a car parked on the drive of one house, but, although Olivia's spirits lifted, it was the house next door to the Barlows. Still, she was here now. It was worth taking a chance.

It was as she was locking the car that she looked up and saw Louise watching her. She was standing at the bedroom window, staring down at her visitor, as if she didn't quite believe her eyes.

Olivia didn't attempt a smile, but merely nodded before walking up the open-plan drive to the house. And, by the time she reached the door, Louise had it open, her expression mirroring the obvious agitation she was feeling.

'Well,' she said tersely. 'You've got a nerve!'

Olivia blew out a breath. 'May I come in, or do you want to discuss Sean out here?'

Louise's lips tightened. 'You'd better come in,' she said, albeit unwillingly. 'I just hope nobody recognises your car.'

'It's a rental,' said Olivia flatly, following the other woman across a narrow hall and into a pleasant sitting room. Then, noticing how pale Louise was looking, she added, 'I'm sorry if I've upset you, but Joel should have told you what he was going to do.'

'Yes, he should.' Louise nodded to a chair. 'You'd better sit down and tell me why he isn't looking after Sean himself.'

Olivia sighed. 'The tutor who was going to cover his lectures has broken his hip.'

'So why didn't he tell me he couldn't have Sean and been done with it?'

'You'll have to ask him that.' Olivia hesitated. 'I assume because he didn't want to disappoint the boy.'

'And I dare say he was glad of any excuse to ask you to help him out,' said Louise scathingly. 'If it wasn't so embarrassing, it would be pitiful!'

'Actually, it wasn't like that,' said Olivia, taking the seat she'd been offered and crossing her legs as if she was completely at her ease. 'Did he tell you I found Sean after he'd spent the night in our barn?'

Louise sagged a little, and then sank onto the sofa opposite. 'It was you who found him!' she exclaimed. 'No, I didn't know that. Joel just said someone had found him and Sean had insisted on being taken to Millford.'

'Well, it was me.' But Olivia was feeling concerned now. Louise did look incredibly white and exhausted. 'I— we—he did insist on speaking to his father. And I have to admit, I was pretty peeved that you apparently hadn't even noticed he was missing.'

Louise nodded. 'I suppose it did look bad,' she admitted in a much less confrontational tone. 'But he had run away just a few days before, and I've been feeling so—well, so sickly, I suppose I didn't give it the significance it deserved.'

Olivia frowned. 'You've been ill?'

'No.' Louise flushed. 'Just a bit under the weather, that's all.'

'And you assumed Sean had gone to Joel's again?'

'Yes.' Louise pushed weary hands through her tumbled dark hair and Olivia saw with some concern that she was sweating. 'I suppose you think I'm a bad mother. But Sean's not an easy kid to deal with. Not when he and Stewart don't get on.'

Olivia shook her head. 'It's nothing to do with me, Louise.'

'So you're not going to spread the fact that I neglect my child around the village?'

'No.' Olivia was horrified. 'I came here because I didn't want you to get the wrong impression about Joel and me. He was in a bind and I was—available.' *Oh, God!* 'There's no hidden agenda,' she added hurriedly. 'I'm not trying to cause trouble between you two.'

Louise regarded her curiously. 'You and Joel aren't getting back together, then?'

'Heavens, no!' Olivia was very definite about that.

But even as she said the words, she wondered at the pang of regret that stirred deep in her stomach. Was it possible to want a man you didn't like? She had to believe it was, or face the alternative. That these feelings she couldn't seem to control weren't going to go away.

'I wondered,' Louise was saying now, and Olivia found it very hard to remember their conversation. The other woman pulled a wry face. 'It took him a long time to get over you, you know.'

'Oh, I don't think—'

'It's true.' Louise had evidently decided to be generous now that her own position wasn't threatened. 'I've thought, since the divorce, that he only married me because he wanted to prove to himself—and all the gossips in the village—that he'd moved on; made a success of his life.'

Olivia shook her head. 'Well, thanks for that, but Joel isn't the reason I came here. You probably know, my dad had a stroke and I wanted to come home to see him.' If that wasn't quite the way it had happened, it served the purpose. 'I am thinking of staying on for a while, but just so I can be with the family.'

'All the same—'

'Louise, really, I'd rather you didn't say anything about Joel and me to anyone. You may not know it, but I only came back to England because my second marriage didn't work out either.' She paused, and then, realising she had to say something dramatic to wipe that smug look off Louise's face, she added, 'Bruce and I were together for much longer than Joel and me.'

Louise's eyes widened. 'So you're divorced again?'

'Afraid so.' Olivia got to her feet, trying to sound philosophic. 'Anyway, I'm glad we've had this talk, Louise. I think we understand one another now.'

CHAPTER TEN

OLIVIA parked her car above the dunes and turned off the engine. It was a beautiful evening. It had been an incredibly mild day for early May and, now that the sun was sinking in the west, the sky above Redes Bay was streaked in shades of red and orange and purple.

Reaching into the glove compartment, Olivia pulled out a scrunchie and tugged her hair into a high pony-tail. Then, thrusting open her door, she got out of the car.

She was dressed in just a khaki tank-top and running shorts, and, after checking that her trainers were safely tied, she tucked the car keys into her pocket and set off.

It was weeks since she'd run any distance. When she'd first returned to England she'd contented herself with exercising at the local gym, but there was nothing like running in the fresh air. And today, particularly, she'd needed to get out of the house.

It wasn't that either Linda or Martin had said anything to upset her. On the contrary, during the past week or so, since she'd been ferrying Sean about, they'd been very supportive. In Martin's case, amazingly so, but she still felt as if sooner or later the axe was going to fall.

She had talked to her father about Linda and Martin's ambitions for the farm. It was he who'd brought the subject up and she'd had to admit that she thought it had some merit. But Ben Foley was opposed to letting strangers have free use of his land, even if he could offer no other solution to the problem.

Nevertheless, Olivia enjoyed the time she spent with the old man. Unlike the rushed awkward encounters she had with Joel, she and her father had long conversations about everything under the sun. She'd even told him about Bruce and why he hadn't wanted her to leave him. And discovered that the pain of that betrayal no longer had the strength to hurt her.

Her relationship with her first husband did not progress so easily, however. Not that she saw a lot of Joel really. He was there to say goodbye to his son in the mornings. And on those occasions when she was obliged to stay with Sean until his father got home in the evenings, she'd usually got her coat on before he'd got out of the car. Their exchanges were brief and always subjective. They spoke of Sean, of any conversations she'd had with Sean's teachers, and little else.

On the other hand, she and Joel's son had become much closer. Indeed, she was dreading the time when he would have to go back to his mother. It was almost two weeks now, but talk of his return hadn't been mentioned yet, and Olivia was hoping that Joel would be granted a stay of execution.

Tonight she hadn't been needed, however. Sean had gained permission from his father to spend the night at his best friend's house. They were having a sleepover, Sean had told Olivia that morning, full of excitement at the thought of the midnight feast they were planning. She wouldn't be needed in the morning either, because the other boy's mother would take them both to school.

Now Olivia stopped at the edge of the dunes, doing some warm-up exercises before stepping down onto the sand. She intended to run along the shoreline where the sand was damp and firm. Then she might call in the pub for a cool drink before heading back.

Drawing one knee up to her chin and then the other, she felt a rising sense of anticipation. Running had always given her a feeling of freedom, of the confidence she could have in her own muscles, her own strength.

And then she saw him. He was doing what she had planned to do, running along the shoreline, pounding the sand in a steady pace, long strides stretching long, powerful legs.

Joel!

Olivia blew out an impatient breath. Wouldn't you know it? she asked herself. Two minds with but a single thought. Why hadn't she considered that he might take advantage of his freedom? Redes Bay had always been a favoured spot for both of them.

She would have turned away then, but he'd seen her. There was a moment when he faltered, when she was sure he would simply acknowledge her with a lift of his hand perhaps and go on. Contrarily, he didn't do either of those things. He stopped for a moment, and then jogged towards her. What now? she wondered uneasily. She hoped he didn't think she was following him.

For all that, she couldn't help watching him as he drew nearer. A grey tank-top clung damply to the contours of his chest and his arms bulged with muscle. Tight-fitting cycling shorts did nothing to hide his maleness, and with sweat beading his forehead he looked big and impressively virile.

'D'you want to join me?' he asked, surprising her. He was closer now, but remained on the damp sand, jogging on the spot, not allowing his body to cool down.

'I—well, if you don't mind,' said Olivia, stepping over the soft sand and testing the damp sand for its firmness. 'Do you often run here?'

'Why? So you can avoid it in future?' Joel asked drily, realising he had probably made a mistake by inviting her company. But the beach was free to all, for goodness' sake, and he'd sensed that if he hadn't spoken she'd have abandoned her run.

'No.'

Olivia's response was defensive, and, breaking away from him, she jogged away along the beach. She took it slowly at first, only increasing her pace when she felt the muscles in her legs loosen and the adrenalin started flowing through her body.

Joel let her go, let her get some distance ahead of him, knowing that in a few loping strides he'd overtake her. As he watched her, however, he felt his body tighten. In the skin-tight tank-top and running shorts, she was every man's wet dream come true and heaven knew he wasn't immune to her appeal.

She was so sexy, that was the problem. Long, slim arms and legs; hips that swelled into the provocative curve of her bottom. She might not have been aware that her breasts had puckered when he'd challenged her, but he was. Distinctly upturned, they'd pushed delicately against the cloth of her vest.

Hell!

He saw her glance back over her shoulder then and guessed she was wondering if he'd changed his mind about them running together. He should, he acknowledged grimly. But although his brain might protest his recklessness, his flesh was shamefully weak.

Picking up his pace, he went after her and seconds later he came alongside her. She was running smoothly now, taking long, ground-covering strides, her breasts bobbing rhythmically beneath the tank-top.

They ran in silence for a while, but then Joel saw the line of dampness appearing in the small of her back. 'Don't overdo it,' he warned, feeling obliged to remind her that, unless he was mistaken, she hadn't done any running since she'd come to Bridgeford.

'I'm OK.' Olivia spoke breathily. 'It's a beautiful evening, isn't it?'

'Beautiful,' agreed Joel, dragging his eyes away from her and looking towards the horizon. 'On evenings like these, it feels as if it's going to stay light forever.'

'I know what you mean.' Olivia was relieved that he seemed prepared to meet her halfway. 'At this time of year, you don't want to go to bed.'

Joel couldn't help himself. 'I suppose that depends who you're going to bed with,' he remarked wryly, and Olivia gave him an impatient look.

'You had to say that, didn't you?'

Joel arched mocking brows. 'Well, you asked for it.'

Olivia shook her head. 'Must you bring sexual innuendo into everything? Is that what comes of mixing with amorous adolescents like that girl I saw at your office?'

Joel stifled a laugh. 'Oh, Liv, have you any idea how prudish you sound?' He turned, running backward so he could see her face. 'For your information, Cheryl Brooks is twenty-four. She's already a graduate and working towards her second degree.'

'Bully for her.' Olivia resented the ease with which he was keeping up with her. 'In any case, she's too young for you.'

Joel gasped. 'Did I say she wasn't?'

'No, but as you were talking about taking women to bed—'

'I wasn't talking about any such thing.' Joel was indignant. 'You brought it up, Liv. Not me.'

'Whatever.'

Olivia could feel her legs beginning to tire. She'd passed the pain barrier some minutes ago, but now it was becoming a distinct effort to keep putting one foot in front of the other. However, she wasn't going to let Joel get the better of her in this as well as everything else, and, making an especial effort, she quickened her pace until she was actually pulling away from him.

The pain was excruciating, her knees burning as if they were on fire. But there was such satisfaction in besting him that she could actually numb her mind to the agony in her legs.

It didn't last. As soon as he realised what she was doing, Joel quickened his own pace and within seconds he'd caught up with her.

'Crazy woman!' he exclaimed, one look at her contorted face enough to tell him that she was in danger of doing some permanent damage to herself. He put a restraining hand on her arm, feeling the trembling muscles,

the sweat that was streaming out of her. 'For heaven's
sake, Liv, you're going to kill yourself!'

Olivia sagged. She couldn't help it. Even the warning
touch of his hand was too much, and, stumbling, she fell
to her knees on the sand.

'Liv, are you all right?'

Instantly abandoning any thought of continuing his
own run, Joel came down on his haunches beside her, one
hand on the back of her neck, the other gripping her
upper arm, supporting her when she would have sunk
onto the sand. Despite his own exertions his hands were
cool and firm, and, unable to help herself, Olivia slumped
against him.

'For pity's sake!'

Joel swore to himself, looking about him as if assistance
was going to materialise by magic. But there was no one
else on the beach. And they were some distance from
where they'd left their cars. Part of the beauty of Redes Bay
was its absence of human habitation. Apart from the pub,
that was, but that was some distance away, too.

'I'll—I'll be all right in a minute.'

Olivia spoke faintly, still struggling to regulate her
breathing. Her lungs burned and it was incredibly difficult
to take the gulping breaths she knew she needed to recover.
She was beginning to feel cold, too, the breeze off the
North Sea picking up as night drew in.

She shivered and Joel felt it. Dammit, she was going to
develop hypothermia if he didn't get her warm soon. There
was no way she was going to be able to walk back to her
car in her present condition. He was going to have to leave
her here and go and get help on his own.

He hesitated a moment, aware that his tank-top was rank with his own sweat, but then he pulled it over his head and wrapped it about her shoulders like a shawl. 'Stay there,' he said, and when she tried to protest he held the top tighter about her. 'I won't be long,' he promised grimly. 'Please, Liv. Just stay here until I get back.'

'But—you'll get cold,' she protested, and he managed an ironic grin.

'I don't think so,' he said, getting to his feet in a swift, lithe movement. 'Baby, just looking at you burns me up. Now, be good. I won't be long.'

Olivia had managed to get to her feet and was taking several tentative steps across the sand when she saw the Lexus barrelling towards her. For the first time in her life, she appreciated the advantages of having a four-wheel-drive vehicle. Its huge tyres ate up the beach as if it was the smoothest highway, only the spray of sand behind showing its passing.

Joel braked beside her and sprang out. He'd evidently found a T-shirt to cover his bare chest that Olivia had admired so briefly and in his hands he carried a sheepskin jacket that he quickly exchanged for the ratty tank-top. Feeling the comfort of the jacket envelop her, Olivia began to feel warmth radiating inside her, the spasmodic shivers that had racked her fading swiftly with its heat.

'Come on.'

Not giving her a chance to object, Joel swung her up in his arms and carried her to the Lexus. Swinging open the passenger-side door, he lifted her into the seat, pausing long enough to secure the safely belt before circling the bonnet and getting in beside her.

'Better?' he asked, looking sideways at her, and she nodded her head.

'Much.' She moistened her lips. 'Thanks.'

Joel didn't make any response. He just held her gaze for a few moments longer and then, thrusting the Lexus into drive, he did a U-turn and drove back to where the vehicle had carved a path across the dunes.

However, when they were safely on the coast road again, he didn't take her back to where she'd left her car. Instead, he turned up the cliff road, negotiating the precipitous bends with admirable speed.

Olivia looked at him then, and, feeling her eyes on him, he said, 'You're not fit to drive yourself home right now. Your body's had a shock. You need to chill out before you get back behind the wheel of a car.'

'Perhaps so.' Olivia blew out a breath. 'But I am feeling much better now.'

'That's good.' Joel was approving. 'But you don't realise how exhausted you are. What you need is a long, hot shower and a cool glass of wine. That's my recommendation anyway.'

Olivia's lips tightened. 'Yeah, right,' she said drily, wondering what Linda would say if she used all the hot water. 'I'll—think about it.'

'We'll do better than that,' said Joel blandly, and, blinking, Olivia realised something that she should have noticed minutes ago. She was so used to driving to Millford these days that she hadn't questioned the route they were taking. But now comprehension dawned.

'This isn't the way to Bridgeford!' she exclaimed, her tongue adhering to the roof of her mouth. 'Joel, I can't go to your house.'

'Why not?' Joel was complacent. 'You spend a couple of hours there most days. You must be quite familiar with it by this time.'

Olivia shook her head. 'That's different.'

'I know. Sean's there. And he provides a chaperon. But that doesn't mean we need one, does it?'

Doesn't it? For a moment, Olivia thought she'd said the words out loud, but Joel hadn't responded so she knew she'd only been thinking them. But, dear God, going to Joel's house late in the evening, using his shower! Wasn't that just asking for trouble?

Joel parked the car at his gate and without waiting for his assistance Olivia thrust open her door. But her legs felt like jelly when she climbed down from the seat and she couldn't decide whether it was exhaustion or anticipation.

'Here, let me help you,' he said, but Olivia lifted a warning hand to keep him at arm's length.

'I can manage,' she said, with more confidence than she was feeling. But she could just imagine the Reverend Webster's reaction if he saw Joel carrying her into his house.

Joel opened the door and, unwillingly, Olivia stumbled up the path and into the house. It was all familiar, yet strangely unreal. For the first time since that afternoon in his office, they were alone together.

Joel closed the door with his foot and looked at her. Then, when Olivia evaded his gaze, he dropped the tank-top he'd been carrying onto the floor and walked across to the stairs. 'Can you make it?' he asked, indicating the climb, and Olivia took a deep breath.

'If you think that what we're doing is wise,' she said at

last, trudging across the floor. 'What if Louise finds out? Aren't you worried that she might use it against you?'

Joel rested one hand on the newel post at the foot of the staircase. 'The way I heard it, you apparently put her in her place. And why should she care what I do? It's not as if Sean's a witness to my depravity.' He regarded her impatiently. 'Come on, Liv. You're wasting time and I'm getting cold.'

'Oh—sorry.' Olivia made a helpless gesture, indicating that he should go first. Although she'd been upstairs before and had a pretty good idea where Joel's bedroom was, she had no intention of letting him know that. 'Go ahead.'

Despite her determination not to show any weakness, it was an effort going up the stairs. By the time she reached the landing, she was panting again and she had to acknowledge how out of condition she was. But to her relief Joel chose not to call her on it, and, walking across the gallery, he opened the door into one of the spare rooms.

'You can use the bathroom in here,' he said, his voice cool and objective. 'Take as long as you like. You'll find plenty of towels on the rack.'

'Thanks.'

Olivia moved past him into the bedroom, admiring the gold satin counterpane on the colonial-style bed. There were gold and green patterned curtains at the windows and a carved *armoire* where one could store clothes. The carpet underfoot was a cream shag pile, its softness evident even through her shoes.

She turned to say how much she liked his style of decoration, but Joel was gone. He'd closed the door silently and left her, and she beat back a sudden surge of disappointment. This was what she wanted, wasn't it? she asked herself: their relationship to remain on civil terms. She felt tonight had proved that friendship was out of the question. She was much too aware of the pitfalls she faced when she tried to be sociable with him.

The bathroom was delightful. A claw-footed tub flanked a glass-walled shower cubicle, with twin basins matching the low-level lavatory. A rack of towels occupied the wall beside the shower and Olivia didn't hesitate before stripping off her tank-top and shorts and stepping into the cubicle.

Unlike at the farm, it was a power shower, and, feeling the hot spray massaging her shoulders, pummelling her hips, shedding its heat all over her body, she felt her exhaustion easing into a healthy tiredness. It was so good to feel thoroughly warm again, inside as well as out, and, finding a tube of shampoo on a ribbed shelf inside the cubicle, she decided to wash her hair as well.

She left the shower with real regret. It had been so wonderful to wash herself without the ever-present prospect of being disturbed hanging over her head. And, although it was satisfying to feel clean again, she was sorry it was over.

She dried herself rapidly. There was no lock on the bathroom door and, though she doubted that Joel would intrude on her here, she was intensely aware of her nakedness.

That was why, when there was a knock at the bathroom door, there was a rather ungainly scramble to get the towel wrapped securely about her before she spoke.

CHAPTER ELEVEN

'Yes?' she called, her voice sounding absurdly weak and thready. What could he possibly want?

'I've left a robe on the bed,' Joel responded equably. 'If you'd like to put it on and bring your running clothes downstairs, I'll put them in the washer with mine.'

'Oh.' Olivia swallowed, thinking hard. But, although she knew that accepting his offer would inevitably delay her departure, the idea of wearing dirty clothes when she felt so deliciously clean swung it for her. 'OK,' she agreed. 'I'll do that. Thanks again.'

'No problem.'

She waited until she heard the outer door close behind him before venturing a peek into the adjoining room. Sure enough, a white towelling bathrobe was lying on the bed, along with a pair of chunky white athletic socks she could wear instead of her trainers.

Giving her hair one last rub with the towel, Olivia combed it with her fingers before sliding her arms into the sleeves of the bathrobe. It was much too big. Joel's, she guessed, though she chose not to dwell on that. Fastening the belt tightly about her waist, she pulled on the socks, also too big, and collected her dirty clothes.

Even if she hadn't known the way to the kitchen, the delicious smell of food would have guided her. Someone, Joel obviously, was preparing his evening meal, and the mingled scents of frying meat and sautéed vegetables drifted up the stairs.

Her feet making no sound in the chunky socks, Olivia padded downstairs and across the hall. Joel was standing at the Aga, stir-frying the food in a rather professional-looking wok. Like her, he'd evidently had a shower, because there were droplets of water sparkling on his dark hair and trickling down into his collar at the back.

Her mouth drying at the sight of him in faded jeans, unbuttoned at the waist, and a short-sleeved shirt that was open down his chest, Olivia knew she had to say something before he caught her watching him. 'I didn't know you could cook,' she said, recalling her own early disasters in that direction. She crossed the tiled floor and peered over his shoulder. 'It certainly smells good.'

Joel started. He'd not been aware of her approach, and his eyes darkened at the picture she made in his robe and socks. Judging by the bundle of clothes in her arms, he was fairly sure she had nothing on under the terry-towelling, and the sudden urge to find out was hardly a surprise in his present mood.

'It's just steak and vegetables,' he said, his voice harsher than it should have been. 'Are you hungry?'

Olivia took a backward step away from him. She was realising that this was hardly keeping her distance, as she'd planned to do when she was upstairs. 'Oh—don't worry about me,' she mumbled awkwardly. 'I—er—I'll just wait until the clothes are dry and then I'll go.' She indicated the bundle in her arms. 'Shall I put these in the washer? It's in the utility room, isn't it?'

'Don't you know?'

Joel growled his answer, but he wasn't feeling particularly charitable right now. Earlier on, going into his spare bedroom, knowing she was naked in the next room, had left him with a hard-on he could do without. But, dammit, his body ached with the need to bury itself in her, the memory of how it used to be between them never totally fading away.

'I suppose I do,' she replied a little stiffly now, moving past him to the outer door. 'I assume you've put yours in already.'

'Yeah.'

Jake gave the stir-fry a vicious shake, unable to prevent his eyes from following her slim form. She'd been right, he thought irritably. This had not been the wisest move he'd ever made.

He heard her close the washer and then the unmistakable sound of running water as she turned the machine on. She came back into the kitchen, carefully averting her eyes as she shut the utility-room door, and his temper erupted. This was crazy, he thought angrily. They were acting as if they were strangers. Intimate strangers, perhaps, but with an atmosphere between them you could cut with a knife.

Taking the pan off the heat, he spun round to face her. 'What is it with you?' he asked savagely. 'I practically save you from pneumonia. I bring you here, to my house, give you free use of my bathroom, offer to wash your clothes and give you half my supper, and what do you do? You say, thanks, but no thanks. I'd rather sit on my own in the other room than share a meal with you!'

'That's not true!' But Olivia's face burned with embarrassment even so. 'I am grateful, truly I am.'

'Well, you have a bloody funny way of showing it.' He raked his nails across his chest where a triangle of dark hair grew between his pectoral muscles and arrowed down to his navel and beyond. 'What did I ever do to make you hate me, Liv?'

Olivia's eyes widened. 'I don't hate you, Joel.'

'What, then?' he demanded, something darker than frustration in his eyes. 'Come on, Liv, tell me what it is you want from me. Because God knows, I'm running out of ideas.'

Olivia shook her head. 'I don't know what you mean.'

'Sure you do.' He was relentless. 'We've tried hostile and neutral. And yes, there have been times when I've stepped over the line. But tonight, I was really trying to be civil. To show you another side to my nature, one you don't seem to believe is there.'

Olivia drew a breath. 'Well, I'm sorry—'

'Yeah, you should be.'

'But you weren't exactly jolly when I came downstairs.'

'You startled me.'

'Did I?' Olivia didn't know where this was going, but she refused to let him walk all over her. 'Or were you in a black mood because you regretted bringing me here? Come on, Joel. Be honest. You made it plain enough before that you didn't want me in your house.'

'*Before.*' Joel latched on to the word. 'That's the pivotal difference. As you've probably been in the house as much as I have the past couple of weeks, it would be freaking crazy to try and bar you from the place now.'

'Ah, but you weren't there when I was, and vice versa,' retorted Olivia at once. 'This isn't the same.'

Joel watched her balefully. She had no idea how he was feeling, he thought, or she wouldn't be standing there, trading put-downs with him. Without make-up of any kind, she was even more desirable than she'd been earlier, her cheeks flushed a becoming shade of pink, her green eyes sparkling with what she thought was a victory.

'You could be right,' he said at last, and although his words were innocent enough, she seemed to sense that he meant something different by it.

'You—you're agreeing with me?' she asked warily and Joel spread his hands.

'That being here alone with you is different from being with Sean? Hey, you'll get no argument from me.'

Olivia gnawed on her lower lip. 'Well—good.'

'No, this is much more interesting,' he said, lowering his arms and shoving his thumbs into his dipping waistband. 'Much more interesting, believe me.'

Olivia swallowed. He saw the jerky movement in her throat, saw the way she gathered a handful of the terry-towelling between her breasts. 'Joel,' she said nervously, her eyes flickering to the opening *V* of his jeans. 'Joel, I thought we understood one another.'

'What's to understand?' He looked at her from beneath lowered lids. 'I think we know one another well enough by now.'

She caught her breath. 'Joel,' she said again, but it was more of a plea now. 'Joel, we can't do this.'

'Can't do what?' He placed one bare foot in front of the other. 'What did I say?'

Olivia backed up a pace. 'You didn't have to say it,' she protested, and once again Joel spread his arms.

'I'm not a mind-reader, Liv,' he said, but this time when he lowered his hands he allowed one finger to hook the belt of the bathrobe. 'Perhaps you'd better lay it out for me.'

Olivia shook her head, aware that she'd have to loosen the belt to escape him. 'I think you know exactly what you're doing.'

'No.' Joel was very definite about that. 'No, you know, I don't. But, damn, I'm beginning not to care.'

'Joel—'

Her voice was plaintive, and Joel's mouth took on a sensual curve. 'Yeah,' he said, using the belt to pull her towards him. 'Yeah, say my name, Liv. Say it like you mean it, 'cos I know you do.'

Olivia tried to hang back, but it was a losing battle and she knew it. When he bent his head and covered her lips with his, she couldn't prevent herself from sinking into him. Joel's lips—Joel's tongue—her world suddenly seemed bounded by the sensual invasion of his kiss, and when he parted the robe and found her breasts her nipples thrust eagerly against his palms.

'Oh, baby,' he groaned, pushing his hips towards her, and, feeling the rough fabric of his jeans against her bare legs, she realised the bathrobe was now completely open. 'I knew you were naked,' he added hoarsely, looking down at her. His teeth nuzzled her ear. 'Do you wonder why I can't fasten my jeans?'

'It's not something I've thought about,' protested Olivia,

not altogether truthfully, and Joel regarded her with smouldering eyes.

'No?'

Olivia quivered. 'Why don't you tell me?' she found herself saying, her voice as unsteady as his. His words had been unbearably sexy and she wanted to prolong the moment. 'Do I—do I turn you on?'

'Why don't you find out for yourself?' he breathed, taking one of her hands and letting her feel the hard ridge that was threatening his zip. 'Do you have any idea how long it is since I was in danger of losing it completely?'

Olivia's tongue circled her lips almost consideringly. Then, averting her eyes, she deliberately loosened his zip so she could slip her hand inside his jeans. He wasn't wearing underwear and when her fingers closed around his thick shaft he bucked violently against her.

'Hell, baby, take it easy,' he groaned, drawing back from her and restoring himself to some semblance of dignity. 'D'you want me to come in your hands?'

'I wouldn't mind.' Olivia realised this had gone too far now for her to pretend. Lifting her hands, she cupped his face, not even thinking about her nakedness. 'But I'd rather you were inside me.' She nudged him provocatively. 'What about you?'

'God!' Joel stared down at her. 'Need you ask?'

'Good.' Without a shred of shame, Olivia tipped the robe off her shoulders, letting it fall in a soft heap about their feet. 'Is this better?'

Joel moved his head a little dazedly. But then the realisation that they were standing in a room that was lit by fluorescent tubes that ran beneath the wall units caused him to utter a muffled curse.

'Not here.' He gripped her waist and lifted her so that she was able to wind her legs about his hips. His voice thickened. 'Let's go upstairs.'

He crossed the hall and climbed the stairs without any visible effort on his part. On the landing, he made straight for his own bedroom. He could have taken her into either of the two spare rooms, but he didn't. He wanted her in his arms in his bed, and, as if she knew how he was feeling, Olivia spread herself invitingly as soon as he laid her on the slub silk coverlet.

'Why don't you lose the socks?' he suggested as he sloughed his shirt and kicked off his jeans and she turned onto her side and lifted first one leg and then the other, making the removal of the socks a deliberate provocation. Her breasts rested full and luscious against the coverlet, the curve of her hips as sleek and smooth as the rest of her.

'You weren't kidding,' she mocked him softly, admiring his erection. 'I do turn you on, don't I?'

'Baby, I've had a hard-on since I saw you doing those sexy moves on the beach,' he told her huskily. He knelt on the bed, rolling her onto her back so he could move over her. Supporting himself on his hands so he didn't crush her, he bent and bit one swollen nipple. 'Did you think I hadn't seen you? Or was it all for my benefit?'

Olivia's lips parted, half in protest, half in delicious pain. 'I was stretching, Joel.'

'And the rest.' Joel transferred his attentions to her other breast and sucked hungrily. 'You knew exactly what you were doing.'

'Yes. I was warming up,' she insisted, catching her

breath at the sudden heat between her legs. 'I didn't even see you at first.'

'Well, I saw you,' said Joel, moving lower to circle her navel with his tongue. 'I couldn't take my eyes off you.'

Olivia quivered, her nails digging into the coverlet at either side of her. 'I'd never have guessed.'

'Liar!'

'No, I mean it.' She took an uneven breath. 'Does that mean you liked what you saw?'

Joel's eyes flicked briefly to her face. 'What do you think?'

Olivia tried to reach for him then, but he evaded her hands, moving lower to part the soft brown curls at the apex of her legs. He watched her as he touched her there, his fingers discovering how wet she was before he bent and replaced them with his lips.

'Joel—'

She shifted feverishly, but Joel wouldn't let her get away. 'You taste incredible,' he said thickly. 'Shall I make you come? You want to. I can tell.'

'I want you,' whispered Olivia helplessly, and he lifted his head and met her tormented gaze.

'I think you do,' he said, his tongue making one last intimate invasion before he moved over her again. 'I want you, too, baby.' He lowered his body onto hers. 'Hmm, that feels so good.'

Olivia clutched his shoulders, winding her fingers into his hair, shifting restlessly beneath him. She parted her legs, trying to show him she was ready, but his sex contin-ued to throb silkily against her thigh.

Joel understood how she was feeling. His body was aching with needs only she could satisfy. His mouth found hers, his breathing hoarse and unsteady. If things were moving too fast, he couldn't control them any longer, and, lifting her legs until her feet were flat against the cover, he pushed his hard length into her slick sheath.

He heard the moan she gave as he entered her, but it wasn't a moan of protest. Her legs were already lifting, winding around him, urging him so deeply inside her that he was sure he touched the vulnerability of her womb.

Then his own needs took over. As he moved, she tightened around him, showing him more clearly than in words how close to the edge she was. Her breasts were crushed against his chest as she arched her body against him, the sensual dance of their mating growing more and more intense.

Olivia's senses were spinning out of control, yet some coherent part of her brain knew that this was Joel she was with, Joel who was inside her; Joel, whose thrusting hips were causing her to experience the kind of wild abandon she hadn't known since the last time they were together.

Sweat was slicking their bodies, and Joel's mouth ravaged hers, his tongue plunging over and over in imitation of his lovemaking. And she clung to him as if she'd never let him go again, as if he was the only safe place in this furious storm of emotion.

When she felt her excitement was in danger of exploding, she tried to control it. She didn't want this to end, didn't want to lose the spiralling delight that Joel was giving her. But it was too hard to hold it back, too tantalising to be restrained by her trembling efforts. Like a fountain, it rose inside her, enveloping her in its heat and sensuality. And, when the peak was reached, she fell through mindless caverns into heavenly space…

Joel felt the racking tremors as they swept over her, knew the moment she climaxed and he was drenched in the heat of her release. It was all he needed to tip him over the edge and his body convulsed almost simultaneously. He spilled his seed helplessly, his limbs shaking long after he was spent. And knew if this was a mistake, it was a doozy. There was no way he could explain this to himself.

CHAPTER TWELVE

HE MUST have fallen asleep because Joel opened his eyes to find soft fingers stroking back his hair from his forehead, trailing down his roughening cheek to his chin. The same fingers continued on over his throat and the muscled contours of his upper chest to where his flat nipples received similar attention.

He didn't know if Olivia knew he was awake or not, but what she was doing was so pleasurable that he didn't want her to stop. He could feel himself hardening from the state of semi-arousal he'd awakened in, and wondered if she knew his jutting sex meant he was fully aware of her ministrations.

Whatever, she didn't look at him, concentrating instead on caressing the hair that grew low on his stomach. Fine and dark, it couldn't compare to the curly thatch that surrounded his erection, and he sucked in a breath when she bent her head and took his length into her mouth.

His blood pressure erupted. He'd thought he was totally spent but one touch of those tempting lips, of that sensuous tongue, and he was as hard as a ramrod. He clenched his fists when he felt her soft breasts swing against his thighs, and stifled a groan when she parted his legs so she could cup him in her hand.

'Oh, Liv,' he muttered then, the sucking motion of her mouth creating an explosive heat he wasn't sure he could contain. The temptation was to let her have her way with him, to pump whatever strength was left inside him into the liquid fire of her mouth.

He was shuddering with the effort of resisting this when she lifted her head and gave him a teasing look. 'Did I do something wrong?' she asked, continuing to caress him. And, when he would have grabbed her shoulders and rolled her over onto her back, she swiftly straddled him.

'My turn,' she said, deliberately lowering herself so that her wet heat burned his thighs. 'Is this what you want?'

'You know what I want,' muttered Joel hoarsely, his hands gripping her knees almost painfully. 'Liv—for pity's sake! Put me out of my misery.'

Olivia smiled then, and Joel was struck by how beautiful she was, more beautiful now than he had ever seen her. 'Oh, all right,' she said with assumed resignation. 'If I must.'

'You—must,' said Joel grimly, and with a toss of her head she lifted herself until the very tip of his shaft was brushing her core.

'Like this?' she asked, unable to deny the breath of satisfaction that issued from her as she impaled herself upon him. 'Yes?'

'Yes,' said Joel, thrusting his head back into the pillow. 'Yes, yes, yes.'

She rode him with a sensual expertise that had him reaching for her breasts, dragging her head down and savaging her mouth with his. And although once again

Olivia would have liked to prolong their pleasure, her body was too finely attuned to his. When he began to buck beneath her, the white-hot heat of her own desires swiftly swept her away.

However, when she sank onto his chest, Joel rolled her over onto her back, and she experienced another orgasm before he allowed himself to share her climax. Totally exhausted, she found she couldn't keep her eyes open, and the last thing she remembered was Joel's heavy weight slumping beside her.

She awakened feeling amazingly refreshed. She didn't know how long she'd been unconscious, but, although it was completely dark beyond the uncurtained windows, she felt as if she'd slept for hours.

She stirred and immediately the lamp was lit next to the bed. And now she saw that Joel was sitting beside her, a glass of white wine in his hand.

'Hey,' he said, leaning over to kiss her, and the hair on his chest tickled her bare breasts. It made her instantly conscious of her nakedness, though someone, Joel apparently, had removed the coverlet and covered her to the waist with a linen sheet.

'Hey,' she answered, responding to his kiss, but then almost immediately drawing away. 'What time is it?'

'About one.'

Joel spoke carelessly, but Olivia was horrified. 'One o'clock?' she echoed. 'In the morning?'

'Well, it looks like the middle of the night,' agreed Joel mildly. 'Here.' He reached for a second glass from the bedside cabinet. 'Have some Chardonnay.'

Olivia ignored the glass. 'I must have slept for hours.'

'A couple of hours,' he conceded, returning the second glass to the cabinet. 'Chill, baby. Linda knows where you are.'

Olivia's jaw dropped. 'She does?'

'Yeah.' Joel took a sip of his wine before continuing. 'I phoned her and explained you'd fallen asleep.' His mouth tilted. 'Of course, I didn't tell her where you'd fallen asleep exactly. I let her think we'd been having a drink after our run and you'd flaked out.'

'Well, thank you.' But Olivia didn't sound grateful. 'My God, Joel, what's my father going to think?'

Joel regarded her steadily. 'If I know Ben, he'll have guessed precisely what we've been doing. He may have had a stroke, Liv, but he's not a fool.'

'I know that.' Olivia levered herself up against the pillows, and then, seeing where his eyes were riveted, she hauled the sheet up to her chin. 'I've got to get back. I can't stay here. No one's going to believe I slept on your sofa all night.'

Joel's eyes darkened. 'Does it matter what anyone thinks?'

'Of course it matters.' Olivia looked anxiously about her. 'You may not care what anyone in Bridgeford thinks of you, but I've got to live there.'

Joel sighed and put his glass aside. 'Stop stressing,' he said, one hand sliding sensuously up her arm to her shoulder. 'Can't we talk about this in the morning?' He nuzzled her shoulder with his lips. 'There's so much I want to say to you.'

Olivia shook her head. 'You don't understand—'

'No, *you* don't understand,' said Joel huskily. 'Do you think you can share what we just shared and walk away?'

His hand curved along her cheek, turning her face towards him. 'I want you, Liv. Not just for one night, but for the rest of my life!'

Olivia sagged back against the pillow. 'You don't mean that.'

'I do.' His lips brushed the corner of her mouth as his hand slid familiarly beneath the sheet she was clutching to her with desperate hands. 'Oh, baby,' he breathed, cupping her breast. 'You must know I never stopped loving you.'

'Joel—'

'No, listen to me,' he persisted urgently. 'Louise knew I didn't love her. Not in the way I'd loved you, anyway. But by the time I'd discovered my mistake, she was expecting my baby. And however much I might regret my second marriage, I'll never regret having my son.'

Olivia moistened her lips. 'I can understand that.'

'Can you?' Joel's hand had found its way between her thighs and she gave a helpless little moan. 'Oh, God, Liv, you don't know how much I wished he was ours. When I first held him in my arms, I wanted him to be our son.'

'Oh, Joel…' Olivia could feel tears burning at the backs of her eyes. It had been such an emotional few hours and hearing him say how he'd felt when Sean was born really tore her apart. 'Thank you for saying that.'

'Don't thank me,' he muttered hoarsely, his mouth seeking hers. 'It's the truth.' He bit her lower lip. 'And maybe you were right to do what you did all those years ago. We were too young—'

'Wait!' Olivia's hand against his chest obviously surprised him, but it gave her the chance to scramble off the bed. Snatching up the silk coverlet, she wrapped it protectively about her. 'What are you saying, Joel? That after everything—everything that's happened, you still think I aborted our child?'

'Liv—'

But his persuasive tone cut no ice with her. 'Answer me, damn you,' she demanded. 'Do you still believe I murdered our baby?'

Joel slumped back against the pillows, resting one wrist across his forehead. 'Don't be melodramatic, Liv,' he said wearily. 'I didn't bring it up to hurt you. I wanted you to know that I've forgiven you—'

'Big of you!'

'—and that as far as I'm concerned that part of our lives is over and forgotten.'

'I haven't forgotten,' said Olivia bitterly. 'How could I forget something that almost destroyed me? *You* almost destroyed me, Joel. You left me, just when I needed you most.'

Joel's hand fell away and he regarded her through heavy-lidded eyes. 'And how do you think I felt when I discovered you'd run away to London rather than face me?'

'I had faced you, Joel.' Olivia was indignant. 'I didn't leave you, Joel. It was you who walked out.'

Joel pushed himself into a sitting position. 'And didn't it occur to you that I might need a little time to get over it?'

'So you went running home to Mummy and Daddy and I bet they didn't advise you to—how would they put it?—give me a second chance.'

'They were as shocked as I was,' retorted Joel, his temper rising. 'They'd thought they were going to be grandparents. How do you think they felt?'

'Well, they never liked me.'

'They thought we were too young to get married, that's all.'

'Then they should have been pleased that we'd split up.'

'Liv—' Once again, Joel tried to appeal to her. Swinging his legs out of bed, he got to his feet. 'We were too young. I accept that now. Can't you just meet me halfway?'

'No!' Olivia stared at him through suddenly tear-wet eyes. 'Joel, I've told you this before, but I'll tell you again. When I found out I was pregnant, I was frightened. Not of having the baby, but of what it might mean to us. You were twenty years old. OK, you were working at the farm, but I knew that wouldn't satisfy you forever. I needed to get a job, a decent job, if only to support you. How was I going to be able to do that with a baby we couldn't possibly afford?'

'Liv—' he tried again, but she wasn't finished.

'I didn't want to lose you,' she said painfully. 'I'd seen how Linda and Martin had had to struggle when they got married. It nearly drove them apart. It wasn't until Martin got that job at the garden centre that they could afford a home of their own.'

'They managed,' said Joel flatly.

'Well, I didn't want that for us. I didn't want us having to live at the farm for years and years. I wanted us to be independent, too. To have a home of our own.'

'So you decided to abort our baby.'

'No!' Olivia was desperate now. 'All right, I did make an appointment at the clinic in Chevingham. I've never denied that. But when I got there I cancelled the appointment. When it came to the point, I couldn't destroy something we'd made together. In love.'

Joel reached for his jeans and started pulling them on.

'I'll take you home,' he said flatly. 'Your clothes should be dry by now. I put them in the dryer when I got the wine.'

Olivia's shoulders sagged. 'You won't listen to reason, will you?'

'Oh, please.' Joel regarded her with scorn in his eyes. 'Your story is that you changed your mind and left the clinic without having the abortion—'

'Yes.'

'And that you had a miscarriage when you got home?'

'You know it is.'

'Bull,' said Joel succinctly. 'You didn't cancel the appointment; you went through with it. And then, when you got home, you cooked up this story about having a miscarriage while there was nobody in the house but you.'

'No!'

'Yes, Olivia. How do you think I found out about the abortion in the first place?' His face contorted. 'You must have thought you were so safe: patient's confidentiality and all that rubbish. You never thought that someone else might care enough to tell me I was being taken for a fool. I've never felt so shattered as I did that day, believe me.'

'But who—?'

'D'you think I'm going to tell you?' Joel shook his head. 'I'll get your clothes,' he said, making for the door. 'And by the way, Sean's going home tomorrow—or rather today. I was going to phone you and thank you for what you've done for him. But it looks like we're all out of explanations, doesn't it?'

CHAPTER THIRTEEN

THANKFULLY, Olivia had a key and when Joel dropped her off she could let herself into the house without waking anyone. But, as she started across the hall to the stairs, she thought she heard someone calling her name. It could only be her father, she thought, making a detour to his room. Pushing the door ajar, she put her head round it, and found Ben Foley propped up on his pillows, as wide awake as if it were the middle of the day.

'Dad!' she exclaimed, pausing a moment to check there was no suspicion of wetness on her cheeks. She sniffed, and moved further into the room. 'What are you doing? You're supposed to be asleep.'

'I sleep a good part of the day,' retorted the old man drily. 'What about you? I thought you were spending the night at Joel's.'

'Linda told you that, I suppose,' Olivia said tightly. 'No. I fell asleep, that's all. When I woke up, he brought me home.'

'So why did he have to bring you home? Where's your car?'

'I left it at the beach.' Olivia made a careless gesture. 'I'd overdone it—running, I mean—and Joel drove me back.'

'To his house.'

'Yes, to his house.'

'Is that why you're looking so tearful now?'

Olivia gasped, rubbing furiously at her eyes. 'I'm not looking tearful.'

'You've been crying,' declared her father steadily. 'You needn't bother to deny it. When a woman's eyes and nose are red, it's a dead giveaway.'

Olivia sniffed again. 'Well, all right. I've been crying. It's not a sin, is it?'

'No.' Ben Foley shook his head. 'But I'd like to know what young Armstrong's done to upset you.'

'Young Armstrong!' Olivia tried to force a laugh. 'Dad, Joel's thirty-five, not nineteen.'

'I'm aware of that.' Her father frowned. 'What's happened? Did you sleep with him?'

'Dad!'

'Don't look at me like that, Livvy. I may be old and crippled, but I'm not numb from the neck down.' He sighed. 'If that man's hurt you, I want to hear about it. He may be thirty-five, but he's not too old to feel the sharp edge of my tongue!'

'Oh, Dad!'

'Well, did you?'

To her dismay, Olivia could feel the tears running down her cheeks again and she fumbled for one of the tissues from the box on the table beside her father's bed. 'I don't want to talk about it, Dad,' she said, scrubbing her eyes again. 'It's late. I ought to get to bed myself.'

'So you did sleep with him,' remarked the old man re-

signedly. 'I knew you would. Sooner or later. But obviously
it didn't work out.'

'Dad!'

'Stop saying "Dad" as if I was a juvenile. You forget
Livvy. I was both mother and father to you for years after
Elizabeth died. All right, it's been some time since we
spent any time together, but I haven't forgotten one small
thing about you. You'll always be my baby, Livvy. The little
girl I had such high hopes for.'

Olivia gripped his hand lying on the duvet beside her.
'Linda told me you had to scrape and save to keep me at
school until I was eighteen,' she said. 'Is that true?'

'Linda had no right telling you any such thing. I was
happy to do what I could. And I'm proud of the way you've
turned out, although you may not believe me. You're a
good woman, Livvy. Caring and generous and too honest
for your own good.'

'What do you mean?' Olivia frowned.

'I mean, all those years ago, telling Joel you'd arranged
to have an abortion. If you hadn't told him that, no one
would have been any the wiser. Miscarriages happen all the
time. Your mother lost a baby just after we got married.
Then we had Linda, without any bother at all.'

Olivia stared at him. 'I didn't know that.'

'Why should you? It's not something most people brag
about. Your mother was very upset, but we got over it.
Things happen!'

Olivia felt a smile tugging at her lips. 'Thanks, Dad,' she
said. 'You've made me feel so much better.' She sniffed
again. 'Is there anything I can do for you before I go?'

'Yes.' Ben Foley's brows drew together. 'You can tell

Linda I've decided to ask the bank for a loan.' He paused. 'Talking to you, being with you, has made me see there's more to life than lying here, waiting for the devil to come and get me. Martin's right. I'm never going to be able to run this place again. Why should I stand in their way? I've got better things to do.'

Olivia caught her breath. 'Like what?'

'Like getting out of this bed, for one thing,' declared her father grimly. 'I'm going to get myself one of those electric wheelchairs, so I can get about by myself. Having that beer the other day reminded me of how long it's been since I had a drink in The Bay Horse. Who knows, maybe some of my old pals won't have forgotten me?'

The following week dragged. Olivia felt emotionally drained, robbed of any sense of optimism about the future. And, although the atmosphere in the house was infinitely more cheerful, now that her father had agreed to approach the bank for a loan, Olivia couldn't see herself staying there any longer than it took to find a place of her own.

It was a situation that had been reinforced by the conversation she'd accidentally overheard Linda and Martin having one evening after they'd thought she'd gone to bed. But she'd been thirsty, and when she'd gone downstairs for a drink she'd heard Martin mention her name.

She hadn't intended to listen. She knew eavesdroppers seldom heard good of themselves. But what she had heard had confirmed her earlier suspicions about her brother-in-law's apparent change of heart where she was concerned.

Martin hadn't changed his mind about her. He hadn't wanted her to stay on at the farm because she was family.

It appeared he'd invited her to stay because he'd been hoping to persuade her to use what little money she had to finance the redevelopment of the cottages, after all. He'd reasoned that without the expense of an apartment, she'd have had no excuse for needing extra funds.

What hurt Olivia the most was that Linda had gone along with it. Obviously her father hadn't known anything abut Martin's manipulations, but Linda had been party to his plans all along. If it hadn't been for her father, Olivia was sure she'd have packed up and gone back to London, the sense of betrayal Joel had awakened only strengthened by her sister's deception.

That was why, a few days later, she found herself in Newcastle again, checking out the estate agents. It served the dual purpose of pricing possible apartments and asking about job vacancies.

She didn't have her CV with her, of course, and it was a very unorthodox way of introducing herself to possible employers. But her experiences in London had taught her that having confidence in her abilities was worth a handful of good references.

Even so, the day was a bit of a disappointment as far as finding herself an apartment was concerned. Those she did view were usually too small or too expensive. The one she did like on the riverside was already spoken for, and she'd had to content herself with leaving her name and phone number just in case the present buyer pulled out of the deal.

Still, she did have a couple of interviews lined up for the following week. She'd have to take a trip to London before that to arrange to have the rest of her belongings couriered north. She'd also check out of the small hotel where she'd stayed when she'd first returned to England. The manager there had offered to keep a room free for her until her return.

On impulse, when she left Newcastle she drove back to Bridgeford via Millford. She assured herself she wanted to see the village again, but the truth was she wanted to drive past Joel's house one more time. She didn't expect to see him. It was the middle of the afternoon and he'd probably be lecturing. In any case, there was no point in pursuing their relationship. Whatever excuses he came up with, she'd never forgive him for not believing her.

She slowed as she reached the green. If Joel's car was at his gate, she was prepared to do a U-turn. But it wasn't. As anticipated, the house looked deserted. Well, what had she expected? But it proved how much she was deceiving herself.

She was driving round the green when she saw Sean. He wasn't on his own. He was walking beside a tall, lanky individual who, despite the fact that he wasn't wearing his cassock, was unmistakably the vicar of All Saints Church.

Olivia hesitated, slowing behind them, not sure what she intended to do until she'd pulled alongside. Then, rolling down her window, she said, 'Hi there,' including them both in her deceptively casual greeting.

'Olivia!' Sean recognised her at once, leaving his relative's side to put both hands on the rim of the open window. He gave her a wistful look. 'I've missed you, Olivia. Have you missed me?'

Olivia wasn't sure how to answer that one. Of course she'd missed the boy, but saying so wasn't going to help anyone. However, Brian Webster saved her the dilemma.

'Oh, it's you, Livvy,' he said without enthusiasm. 'What are you doing in Millford? Joel's not here.'

Olivia could have said that she hadn't come to see Joel, but she didn't. Instead, she turned her attention to the boy. 'Does your mother know you're here, Sean?' she asked, with a swift glance at Brian. 'I thought it was only weekends that you spent with your dad.'

'You're right. He shouldn't be here,' agreed Brian, without giving the boy time to reply. 'He evidently expected to find Joel at home, but he was disappointed. Fortunately, I'd seen him getting off the bus, so I intercepted him before he found somewhere to hide.' He sighed. 'I mean, he could have been hanging about for hours.'

'That's true,' said Olivia, giving Sean a disapproving look. She was remembering what had happened the last time he'd run away and she knew Joel wouldn't be pleased at his reckless disregard of his mother's feelings.

'Well, it is Thursday,' Sean protested. 'And I am supposed to be spending the weekend with Dad. What does it matter if I come a day early?'

Olivia and Brian exchanged glances, and then she said, 'You know the answer to that as well as I do. You're supposed to wait until Friday so your dad can collect you.'

'And let's not forget your mother!' exclaimed Brian. 'She must be out of her mind with worry by now. I'm going to go straight into the vicarage and ring her to let her know where you are. Then I suppose I'll have to drive you home.'

'I don't want to go home,' muttered Sean stubbornly, but Olivia steeled her heart against him.

'I can take him back,' she said instead, immediately regretting the impulse to get involved again.

'Oh, could you?' Brian's face cleared for the first time since she'd met them. 'That is kind of you, Livvy. I've got a wedding rehearsal at five o'clock and I was thinking I'd have to put them off.'

'But I don't want to go home,' said Sean again; however, Brian had no sympathy.

'You don't have a choice,' he said briskly. 'Come along. Get into the car.'

Sean looked sulky. 'I don't have to. Mum says I should never get into a car with a stranger. I can get the bus back. I'm old enough.'

'Get in,' said Olivia warningly, leaning across the passenger seat and pushing the door open. 'Now.'

Heaving a sigh, Sean obeyed her, flopping into the seat beside her with evident ill grace. Brian slammed the door, raising his hand to both of them, and then Olivia put the car in gear and drove away.

'Dad isn't going to like this,' said Sean eventually, apparently deciding to take a different approach. 'He said we wouldn't be seeing you again. Ever. I think he's angry with you. Have you done something to upset him? He wasn't in a good mood all last weekend.'

Olivia gave a brief shrug of her shoulders. 'I'm sure in this instance he'll be glad you're not spending another night in the barn, don't you?'

'I wasn't going to spend the night in the barn.' Sean was indignant. 'I was just going to go and play football on the lawn until Dad got home.'

'And what about your mother?'

Sean sniffed. 'Dad would have rung her when he got back.'

'But what if he had an evening lecture? It could have

been eight or nine before he came home. Your mother would have been frantic by then.'

'No, she wouldn't.'

'Yes, she would.'

'She wasn't before.'

'That was different. She thought you were at your Dad's.'

'But I wasn't.'

'No. But she didn't know that. And as that's where you'd gone before…' Olivia sighed. 'You know I'm right, Sean. You can't keep running away like this.'

Sean hunched his shoulders. 'I wish I could live with Dad.'

'Yes, I think we all know that. But you can't.'

'Why can't I?'

'Because your father isn't married. He doesn't have a wife to look after you when he's not there.' She took a breath. 'If he was married, it would be different. But he's not.'

Sean looked thoughtful. 'You like my dad, don't you?'

Olivia knew where this was going. 'Yes. But I don't want to marry him.'

And how true was that?

'Why not?'

She hesitated, and then, deciding it was now or never, she said, 'Because I was married to him years ago. Before I went to America.' She gave him a rueful smile. 'It didn't work out.'

Sean gazed at her in amazement. 'You were married to Dad,' he said incredulously. 'He didn't tell me that.'

'No, and probably I shouldn't either,' murmured Olivia uneasily. 'But—well, it's not a secret.'

Sean was thinking hard. 'So you must have liked him once,' he said at last, and Olivia stifled a groan.

'It was all a long time ago,' she said quellingly. 'I'd rather talk about why you keep running away from home.' She paused. 'What's wrong? Jo—your dad said you seemed happy enough in the beginning.'

Sean shifted in his seat. 'It was all right, before—'

He broke off and Olivia glanced quickly at him. They'd been here before, too. 'Before—what?' she prompted. 'Go on.'

Sean cast her a look out of the corners of his eyes and then he seemed to slump lower in his seat. 'Before—before the hulk told me they were going to have a baby,' he muttered in a low voice, and suddenly everything he had done made a peculiar kind of sense.

Olivia sought for an answer. 'Well—that's wonderful,' she said at length. 'You're going to have a brother or sister. You should be pleased.'

'So why hasn't Mum told me?' demanded Sean, startling her by his vehemence. 'She hasn't even mentioned it and I don't know if Stewart's lying or not.'

Olivia was beginning to understand a little more. 'Oh, I think it's true,' she ventured gently, remembering Louise's sickness and how pale she'd looked that morning Olivia had called at the house. 'Perhaps she doesn't know how to tell you. Perhaps she's afraid you'll be angry. And what with you running away and all, she probably thinks it's the last thing you want to hear.'

'But—' Sean stared at her. 'But that's why I've been running away. Well, partly, anyway. I'd still rather live with my dad, but that's not going to happen, is it?'

'Not yet,' said Olivia, forcing a smile, wondering how she'd feel if Joel found someone else. Hearing about his marriage to Louise had been painful enough, but at least she hadn't been around to witness it.

Sean frowned. 'So—do you think if I told her I knew she'd be pleased?' he asked consideringly.

'I'm sure of it.' Olivia spoke firmly, wishing her own problems could be solved so easily. 'I think you've got to be grown-up about this, Sean. You're not a baby, are you?'

'No.'

'So, show your mum that you love her; that you'll go on loving her even if she has half a dozen babies!'

The following morning, Olivia was in her father's room, helping him into his wheelchair preparatory to wheeling him to the car, when Linda appeared in the doorway.

'You've got a visitor,' she said without preamble. 'Can you come?'

'A visitor?'

For a heart-stopping moment Olivia wondered if it was Joel, come to thank her for taking Sean home, but Linda soon disillusioned her. 'It's Louise Web—I mean, Barlow,' she said irritably. 'Do you know what she wants?'

Olivia could guess, but she only shook her head. She'd dropped Sean at the end of the road, allowing him to explain where he'd been to his mother if he wanted to. She'd thought it would be easier if he wasn't forced to say what he'd been doing, but if Louise was here it looked as though he'd told her the truth.

'I won't be a minute, Dad,' she said, settling the old man in his chair with an apologetic grimace. 'You can come through, if you like.'

'No, you go and talk to her, Livvy. I'll have another look

at the crossword. And don't worry about me,' he warned her. 'If there's one thing being confined to a bed teaches you, it's patience.'

Linda had put Louise in the living room, and, although she hovered in the doorway for a moment as if she'd have liked to know what the woman wanted, eventually common courtesy forced her to withdraw.

Olivia looked at Louise a little warily when they were alone. 'Linda said you wanted to see me,' she said, gesturing towards the sofa. 'Why don't you sit down?'

As she did so, Olivia noticed that Louise looked much better this morning. There was colour in her cheeks so whatever this was about, it couldn't be all bad.

'I hope you don't mind me coming here,' she said, apparently understanding the situation with Linda. She waited until Olivia had seated herself on the armchair opposite, before she continued, 'First of all, I want to thank you for bringing Sean home yesterday afternoon.'

'That's OK.' Olivia was relieved. 'I'm glad he told you.'

'He had to anyway.' Louise pulled a wry face. 'Brian called me just after you left Millford.'

'Ah.'

'But that wasn't all he told me,' Louise went on, smoothing a hand over the knee of her trousers. 'He told me he knew about the baby; that Stewart had told him without mentioning it to me.'

Olivia nodded. 'I see.'

'It was because he'd talked it over with you, wasn't it? Why is it that he always seems to find it easier to talk to someone else and not to me?' She sighed. 'Still, I suppose I have been pretty wrapped up in myself since I started this morning sickness. I didn't have any with Sean, you see, so I've taken badly to it.'

Olivia didn't know what to say. She and Louise were hardly likely to be friends. 'And was he pleased?' she asked, choosing the least controversial option. She didn't even want to think about how it was when Louise was expecting Sean. That was much too much information.

'I think he is pleased, yes,' Louise said now. 'He thought I didn't want him to know.'

'Well, I'm glad it's turned out so well,' said Olivia, wincing at her choice of vocabulary. 'He's a really nice boy. And a credit to you.'

'Yes, he is. A nice boy, I mean.' Louise blew out a breath. 'Does Joel know? About the baby?'

'Not from me,' said Olivia flatly.

'You don't think Sean might have confided in his father?'

'I think he was worried about you,' said Olivia carefully. 'Staying with his father allowed him to put it out of his head.'

'Well, I appreciate what you did.' Louise bent her head. 'Particularly after the way I behaved.'

'Like you said, you had other things on your mind,' said Olivia, wishing this conversation was over. She made to get to her feet. 'But now, if you don't mind—'

'Wait!' Louise put out a hand, making Olivia stay in her seat. 'I haven't finished.' She wet her lips. 'When I said after what I'd done, I wasn't talking about Sean, Livvy. I was talking about Joel.'

'Joel?'

Olivia was totally confused. What on earth was Louise saying? Unless… The bile rose in the back of her throat.

Unless Louise was about to tell her that the child she was expecting was Joel's.

'I'm not explaining myself very well,' Louise went on uncomfortably. 'But this isn't easy, Livvy.'

Olivia frowned. 'What isn't easy?'

'It was me,' said Louise quickly. 'I was the one who told Joel you'd had the abortion. Maureen—my cousin Maureen, that is—used to work at the clinic in Chevingham. She knew how I felt about Joel, how jealous I'd always been of you. She couldn't wait to tell me that you'd made an appointment and then changed your mind at the last minute.'

Olivia's throat felt dry. 'But you knew I hadn't gone through with it.'

'Yes, but when I heard about your miscarriage, I told Joel that you had.' She hurried on, trying to excuse herself. 'I hated myself afterwards, Livvy. When you two split up and everything. But it was too late then.'

Olivia blinked. 'You destroyed my life because you were jealous!'

'I was totally, totally ashamed of what I'd done.'

'But that didn't stop you from marrying Joel when he came back to Bridgeford, did it?' exclaimed Olivia bitterly. 'My God, Louise, I don't know how you could do such a thing.'

Louise sniffed. 'I know, I know. I was a bitch. And I've paid for it. But—well, I didn't have to tell you,' she added defensively. 'And like I said before, Joel still loved you. So lying to him didn't do me a bit of good.'

CHAPTER FOURTEEN

JOEL emptied his glass and reached for the bottle sitting on the low table in front of him. He upended it into the glass and then scowled when only a few drops of the amber liquid emerged to cover the base of the crystal tumbler. The whisky was all gone. He'd swallowed almost half a bottle of the stuff. Even so, he thought irritably, he should have called at the pub on his way home and bought another. But at that point, he'd still been kidding himself that this wasn't going to be another lousy night.

He flung himself back against the cushions of the sofa, staring unseeingly into the empty grate. It wasn't cold enough to need a fire, but right now he could have done with one. He felt chilled, through and through.

He'd been feeling this way for days, ever since he'd had that phone call from Louise. He'd suspected something was wrong when he'd gone to pick up Sean on Friday afternoon, but he'd assumed she and Stewart had had a row. And then Sean had told him that his mother was expecting a baby, which had seemed to explain her agitation. He knew from the first time she was pregnant that Louise didn't take kindly to losing her figure.

But the call that had come on Sunday evening had been totally out of the blue. After all, it had only been a couple of hours since he'd dropped Sean off, and his first concern had been that there was something wrong with his son. But it had soon become apparent that the reason for Louise phoning him had nothing to do with Sean. What Louise had to say, she hadn't had the nerve to reveal to his face.

To say Joel was devastated by her confession would have been an understatement. He'd wanted to get in his car and drive to Bridgeford and confront Louise personally with her lies. Only the knowledge that Sean would be there, that he might be frightened and not understand his father's anger, had kept Joel from making a scene that night.

However, he had gone to see Louise the following morning. He'd cancelled a lecture and driven straight to his ex-wife's house. He'd been so angry, but she'd been tearful—even though he knew she could turn them on to order—and pregnant, and although he could blame her, the person who was really to blame was himself.

He'd been so stupid. Accepting Louise Webster's story instead of believing his wife. No wonder she'd run away to London. She'd had to suffer the after-effects of the miscarriage without anyone to support her. They'd all believed she was lying. Even her father.

And now, he'd only compounded the offence by showing he still believed she'd had an abortion. That evening they'd spent together had been so perfect until he'd opened his big mouth. He'd thought that by telling her he'd forgiven her, she would be grateful. Instead of which, he'd destroyed their relationship all over again.

He had gone to the farm after seeing Louise, hoping

against hope that Olivia would agree to talk to him. But she hadn't been there. Linda had said her sister had gone to London and she didn't know when—or even if—she'd be back. She had been looking for an apartment in Newcastle, she'd added, but Olivia hadn't found anything she liked.

Which had been the final straw. Joel hadn't slept the night Louise phoned him and he hadn't had a good night's sleep since then. His smug little world had been shattered and he was afraid it was going to take more than a university degree to put it right this time.

When the phone rang, he practically leapt from the sofa to answer it. It might be Olivia, he thought. She could be back from London and Linda would have told her he'd called at the farm.

But it wasn't Olivia. It was his mother, calling from the airport in Newcastle. 'Can you come and pick us up, darling?' she asked. 'The plane was delayed or I'd have rung you earlier. But we wanted it to be a surprise.'

Joel stifled a groan. 'I can't, Mum.'

'You can't?' Diana Armstrong sounded put out.

'No. I'm afraid I've been drinking,' Joel admitted, knowing how that would be received. 'Sorry, Mum. It's good to hear from you, but you should have warned me you were coming.'

Diana mumbled something about thoughtless sons, and then Patrick Armstrong came on the line. 'It's OK, Joel,' he said. 'We can easily take a taxi. It was your mother's idea to ring you. I guessed you might have company tonight.'

Joel frowned. 'Company?'

'What your father's trying so unsubtly to say is that we heard Olivia was back home again,' put in his mother tersely. 'She's not there with you, is she?'

'No.' Joel's tone was cooler now. 'More's the pity. She's not even staying in Bridgeford any longer. Her sister told me she's gone back to London.'

'Well—' Diana was obviously trying not to sound too delighted. 'Well, it's probably all for the best, Joel. After what she did.'

'But that's the point,' said Joel grimly. 'She didn't *do* anything. Louise told me a couple of days ago that she'd been lying when she said Liv had had an abortion. She hadn't. She really had had a miscarriage. And nobody—but especially me—would listen.'

He thought he might feel better when he got off the phone, but he didn't. He'd thought that telling his mother she'd been wrong about Olivia all along would give him some relief. But he was mistaken. The hollowness inside him seemed greater if anything. A great gaping hole of nothingness where once he'd had a heart.

He was in the kitchen, checking for beers in the fridge, when the doorbell rang. He'd just discovered he had two bottles of a German brew and he put them down on the counter with a distinct lack of patience. What now? he thought. Someone selling double-glazing? Or perhaps Sean had run away again. Surely not, now that he knew why his mother had been feeling so unwell.

He hoped it wasn't anyone from the university. He was only wearing drawstring black sweatpants and a black T-shirt. He'd intended to go for a run earlier, but intermittent rain and the bleakness of his mood had deterred him.

It was still light out and when he pulled open the door, he had no difficulty in identifying his caller. Olivia stood outside, slim and beautiful in a red slip dress and incredibly high heels, a loose wrap of some gauzy material floating about her bare shoulders.

'Hi,' she said, sheltering under the lee of the overhang. 'Are you going to invite me in?'

Joel stepped back abruptly, almost losing his balance in his haste to get out of her way. And then, still staring at her as if he couldn't quite believe his eyes, he said stupidly, 'I thought you went back to London.'

'I did.' Olivia moved into the hall, shedding her wrap into his startled hands. Then, glancing thoughtfully at him, she said, 'Are you drunk?'

Joel was taken aback. 'Me?' he said. 'Drunk?'

'You're acting as if you are,' she declared, sauntering past him into the sitting room. Then, turning, she pressed one finger delicately to her nose. 'It smells like a distillery in here.'

Joel tried to pull himself together. 'You're exaggerating,' he said, following her into the room and snatching up the empty bottle and his glass, stowing them away in the drinks cabinet. 'I was having a quiet drink, that's all.'

'A quiet drink?' Olivia faced him, her hips lodged carelessly against the back of the sofa. 'All alone?'

'No, my harem dashed upstairs as soon as you rang the bell,' said Joel shortly. And then, just in case she thought he was serious, 'Of course alone. Who else would I be with?'

Olivia moistened her lips. 'I don't know. What was that girl's name? Cheryl something or other. You could have been with her.'

'No, I couldn't.' Joel took a steadying breath. 'Why are you here, Liv? Have you come to say goodbye?'

'Goodbye?'

'Linda said you might stay in London.'

'Did she? Well, actually, I was arranging to have the rest of my belongings sent to the farm.' She paused. 'Sorry to disappoint you.'

Joel swore. 'That doesn't disappoint me, for God's sake! But what was I supposed to think?'

'Oh, I don't know.' Olivia shifted and the silky bodice moved sensuously against her body. 'You could say you were glad to see me.' She paused. 'You could even say you like my dress.'

Joel groaned. 'You look—fantastic,' he muttered shortly. 'But what is this, Liv? A crucifying mission? Have you come to see how much more pain I can take?'

'No.' Olivia turned then, walking around the sofa, trailing long nails that matched her dress over the soft leather. 'Why should I want to hurt you, Joel? Haven't we hurt one another enough?'

Joel sucked in a breath. 'Then you know—'

'About the lies? Yes, Louise told me.' She glanced his way. 'I assume she's told you?'

Joel nodded.

Olivia moistened her lips. 'And how did that make you feel?'

'Stupid! Devastated! Angry!' Joel raked back his hair with a hand that shook a little. 'God, Liv, I knew Maureen Webster worked at that clinic. And I had no reason to suspect that Louise might be lying.'

'Except that I'd told you it wasn't true!' exclaimed Olivia unsteadily. 'It never occurred to you that I might be telling the truth, did it?'

'Of course it did.' Joel swore again. 'Didn't she tell

you? I phoned the clinic. I wanted proof that you'd actually had an abortion.'

Olivia stared at him. 'And what happened?'

'I got some empty-headed receptionist who said she couldn't give out confidential information about the patients.' He groaned. 'All she would tell me was that, yes, you had had an appointment. She said nothing about you cancelling it.'

'Oh, Joel!' Olivia trembled. 'You should have had more faith in me.'

Joel shook his head. 'Do you think I haven't tormented myself with that ever since Louise decided to tell me?' he demanded. 'I've gone over every minute of those days with a fine-tooth comb and, whatever I do, I can't forgive myself for being such a fool. I should have listened to you. I should have realised you wouldn't have been so upset if it was what you'd wanted. Instead, I could hear the receptionist telling me that you had made the appointment in one ear and Louise whispering that you'd never wanted my baby in the other.'

'Oh, God, Joel—'

'No. Don't feel sorry for me, Liv. I was twenty years old. I should have known better.'

'We were both just kids,' said Olivia huskily, gazing up at him with brimming eyes. 'I wonder if I hadn't run away if we might have learned the truth.'

Joel made a helpless gesture. 'Do you think I haven't considered that, too?' He sighed. 'It would be so easy for me to say that you running away settled the matter. That it proved you'd been lying all along. But I was the real culprit, Liv. I blame myself totally. I moved out of the farm. I let you think that, as far as I was concerned, our marriage was over.'

'Our marriage was over,' whispered Olivia, but Joel only shook his head again, coming towards her, his face dark with emotion.

'Do you honestly think that if you'd stayed in Bridgeford, I'd have been able to keep away from you?' he asked hoarsely. 'For God's sake, Liv, I love you. I've never stopped loving you, dammit. Louise knows that. Maybe that was why she decided to be generous for once in her life.'

Olivia's lips parted, but, although she was tempted to tell him why Louise had had a change of heart, she decided that could wait. Evidently his ex-wife hadn't told him the whole story and Sean wouldn't be too eager to confess that he'd run away again.

'So—what are you saying?' she breathed, running the tip of her finger along the roughened edge of his jawline.

Joel flinched at her touch, but he didn't move away. 'Look at me,' he said instead, gripping the back of his neck with agitated hands. 'You've been back—what? Barely a month. And already I'm a nervous wreck. I can't eat; I can't sleep. And any illusions I had that I was content with my life have all crashed and burned. Does that answer your question?'

Olivia gazed at him. 'You mean that, don't you?'

'Damn right, I mean it,' he declared savagely, and, abandoning any further attempt to restrain his actions, he slid his hands over her shoulders and pulled her against him. 'You know I love you,' he said huskily. 'You must know I want to be with you.' His eyes darkened. 'Does your being here mean that you might forgive me, after all?'

Olivia uttered a breathy little laugh. 'It might,' she said tremulously. 'I'm thinking about it.'

'Well, don't take too long,' said Joel unsteadily, burying his face in the scented hollow of her throat, and Olivia trembled all over.

Her fingers clung to his shoulders, glorying in the taut strength of the arms that encircled her so possessively. Even now, it was hard to let herself believe this was actually happening. She'd been so depressed when she went to London, so unsure of what to think, what to do.

But this was Joel, she thought incredulously, the man she loved and who loved her. Had loved her for fifteen long years, years they'd wasted because of a jealous woman's lies.

And like a dam breaking, emotion flooded her body. There was no need to keep him in suspense. She loved him too much to let this moment slip away. 'I've thunk,' she said huskily, pressing herself against his hard body. 'The answer's yes.'

Their journey up the stairs was only punctuated by moments when Joel divested himself and Olivia of what they were wearing. Her shoes barely made it past the first stair and her dress slipped silkily off her shoulders a few moments later.

The fact that she wasn't wearing a bra caused a few minutes' delay as Joel's hands found her breasts and stroked them into painful arousal. But when she slid her hands beneath his T-shirt, he was compelled to discard it and go on.

She found the drawstring of his sweats only seconds later. The soft fabric skimmed down his narrow hips and he had to kick himself free of them before he tripped. However, her lacy thong did make it to the landing, where it adorned the newel post, like some erotic symbol of their desire.

Their lovemaking was hot and urgent at first. They were hungry for one another and there was no time for foreplay before Joel spread her legs and plunged into her slick sheath. Her moan of satisfaction was stifled by his mouth, and Joel's head was swimming as the blood rushed wildly into his groin.

He felt Olivia climax only moments before his own release, the instinctive tightening of her body engulfing him in flames. 'God, I love you,' he groaned, when he lay shuddering in her arms, and Olivia stroked the damp hair back from his temple with a trembling hand.

'I love you, too,' she whispered. 'So much. As soon as I saw you again, I knew I'd just been kidding myself that I'd got you out of my life.'

They made love again then, gently this time, sharing every delicious moment, stroking and caressing each other in an emotional demonstration of their love and renewal.

But then, Joel propped himself up on one elbow and looked down at her. 'Tell me about Garvey,' he said, not wanting to spoil the moment but he had to know. 'Did you love him?'

Olivia gave a rueful smile. 'Yes, I loved him,' she said. 'But not like I love you,' she added huskily. 'I couldn't understand why at first. He was young and very good-looking and I don't deny I was flattered when he asked me to marry him and move to New York, but there was no real—connection, if you know what I mean?'

'I'm trying to,' said Joel gruffly, and Olivia giggled.

'You've no need to be jealous,' she assured him gently. 'Our relationship was anything but passionate.' She paused. 'I must be incredibly naïve. When he insisted on waiting until we were married before consummating our relationship, I thought he was doing it for me, because he knew I'd had one disastrous relationship—ours—and he thought I wasn't ready for another.'

Joel's brows drew together. 'What are you telling me? That he was—gay?'

'See, you got it in one,' said Olivia ruefully. 'Yes, he was gay. But it took me months before I found out. And because he convinced me that we were good for one another, that it wasn't necessary for a relationship to be a sexual one to work, I went along with it. For what seems like such a long time now.'

Joel turned her face towards him. 'God, Liv, if he hurt you—'

'He didn't.' Olivia sighed. 'I hurt him, I think. But it took me some time to realise that, although I was living this celibate life, Bruce wasn't. I was just his cover, the wife he could escort to functions and display on any occasion when a wife was needed.'

'Hell!'

Joel stared down at her with impassioned eyes and she reached up to press her lips to his. 'Don't look like that, darling. It wasn't all bad. Bruce was a generous man. He was kind. Selfish, perhaps, but kind. I had my own bank account, a string of credit cards. He liked me to spend his money. He encouraged me to fill my wardrobe with expensive clothes, expensive accessories. There was nothing I couldn't have—financially, at least.'

'And then?'

'And then I discovered that he was leading a double life. The nights he was supposed to be working late—he was a merchant banker and they often work late into the evening—he was visiting his lover. Well, a series of lovers, actually,' she appended, her cheeks turning pink. 'He was a member of this club and—'

Joel laid his finger across her lips. 'You don't have to go on,' he said. 'I get the picture.' He paused. 'So you told him you wanted a divorce?'

'Mmm.' Olivia's lids drooped. 'He wasn't pleased.'

'I can believe it.' Joel snorted. 'You were in danger of exposing his deception.'

'Right. And all our friends—*his* friends, and work colleagues, all thought we had an ideal marriage.'

Joel nuzzled her cheek. 'So, what happened?'

'I moved out of our apartment. I got myself a small walk-up in Brooklyn and started divorce proceedings.'

'I gather they took some time?'

'You better believe it.' Olivia nodded. 'Bruce fought me every step of the way.' She bit her lip. 'He—he even went so far as to tell anyone who'd listen that I'd moved out because he wanted children and I didn't. I'd been stupid enough to tell him about—about the miscarriage, and he chose to use that against me, too.'

'But God, you could have made him suffer. Not to mention taking him for every penny he had.'

'I didn't want his money. I didn't want anything from him. OK, maybe I was stupid, but I just wanted to be free.'

'Oh, Liv!' Joel gazed at her with agony in his eyes. 'I wish I could take back every one of those years and make it up to you.'

Olivia looked up then, a smile tilting the corners of her mouth. 'Hey, this is going a long way to achieving it,' she assured him huskily. 'We all make mistakes, Joel. Me more than most.'

'And now?'

She wet her lips with a nervous tongue. 'I suppose that's up to you.'

'OK.' Joel didn't hesitate. Getting up onto his knees beside her, he said, 'Marry me. Marry me, Liv. Again. As soon as I can get a licence.'

'You really want to marry me again?'

'How can you doubt it?' Joel groaned, taking one of her hands and raising her palm to his lips. 'I'm crazy about you, Liv. Say you'll give me a second chance.'

Olivia didn't hesitate either. She wound her arms around his neck and pulled him down to her. 'Oh, I'll give you another chance,' she whispered. 'And I will marry you. Whenever it can be arranged.' She hesitated. 'I want to have your baby, Joel. We can't replace the one we lost, but we can ensure that Sean has more than one brother or sister, hmm?'

They were both sound asleep when the doorbell rang.

Olivia, her bottom curled spoon-like into the curve of Joel's thighs, was the first to hear it. The sound echoed unpleasantly through her subconscious, and, although she didn't want to move, she was obliged to open her eyes and shift a little restlessly against him.

Joel, getting exactly the wrong impression, pressed closer, and she felt the unmistakable stirring of his erection. 'Hey, you're insatiable,' he muttered huskily, parting her thighs, but Olivia pulled away from him, turning onto her back as the doorbell rang again.

'Hear that?' she said, unable to prevent the smile that

touched her lips at Joel's obvious disappointment. 'You've got a visitor.'

'Shit!'

Joel scowled, but when the bell rang for a third time, he had no choice but to slide out of bed and reach for the dressing gown hanging on the back of the bedroom door.

As he wrapped its folds about him, Olivia pushed herself up against the pillows. 'Who do you think it is?' she asked, unknowingly exposing dusky pink nipples to his urgent gaze, and Joel groaned.

'My mother and father?' he suggested flatly, seeing the look of dismay that crossed her face at his words. 'They phoned from the airport earlier. They wanted me to go and pick them up, but, as you know, I'd been drinking. I had to refuse.'

'I'm glad you did,' she murmured, barely audibly, but Joel had heard her.

'So'm I,' he said, pausing to bestow a lingering kiss at the corner of her mouth. 'Hold that thought, baby. I won't be long.'

The bell rang again, more insistently this time, as he went down the stairs, and, although he'd been attempting to pick up all the items of clothing strewn around, the summons was too urgent to ignore. Abandoning his efforts, he dropped the clothes he had rescued onto the chest at the foot of the stairs and strode barefoot to the door.

'Are you aware that it's raining, Joel?' demanded his mother, brushing past him into the hall. 'So much for us being concerned about you. You certainly took your time answering the door.'

'Are you aware that I was in bed, asleep?' retorted Joel,

giving his father an apologetic look as he followed his wife inside.

'In bed?' Diana Armstrong took off her jacket and shook a spray of water over the floor. 'It's barely ten o'clock, Joel. How much have you been drinking, for heaven's sake?'

'It's none of your—'

He didn't finish. His mother had been about to deposit her coat on the chest when she saw the jumble of clothes Joel had dropped there. Without hesitation, she picked them up, saying with obvious distaste, 'You've got a woman here, haven't you? Your father was right.'

Joel took the garments out of his mother's hands and returned them to the chest. 'Not *a* woman,' he said tersely. '*The* woman. Liv arrived just after you'd called. Does that explain the situation?'

Diana's mouth dropped open in disbelief, but Patrick Armstrong was much less perturbed. 'I wondered how long it would be before you two got together again,' he said warmly. 'I hope it works out this time, son. I really do.'

'Thanks, Dad.'

Joel shook the hand his father offered, but Diana wasn't finding it so easy to come to terms with what she'd heard. 'You mean—you were in bed with Olivia Foley?' she said incredulously. 'Oh, Joel, is that wise? What if—what if she hurts you again?'

'I won't.'

The voice came from above their heads and Joel turned to find Olivia coming down the stairs towards them. She was wearing an old rugby shirt of his that barely covered her thighs, a momentary peek of scarlet lace proving she'd rescued her thong from its perch.

His heart leapt into his chest as he went to meet her. She was so adorable, so beautiful, and she was his. He could hardly believe that fate was being kind to him at last. He wanted to take her in his arms and howl his satisfaction to the moon.

'Olivia!' Diana recovered quickly, moving towards the pair of them with a practised smile on her face. 'You must forgive me for being anxious. It's a mother's privilege, you know?'

'Well, it's a wife's privilege to defend herself, Diana,' responded Olivia smoothly, realising that the intimidation Joel's mother had once represented was all gone. 'Hello, Patrick,' she added, accepting his warm hug. 'Did you have a good flight?'

'Well, it was delayed—' Joel's father was beginning, when Diana broke in.

'What did you say?' she demanded. 'A *wife's* privilege?' She turned blankly to her son. 'You two haven't got married again while we were away, have you?'

'Not yet, Mum,' said Joel comfortably, putting a possessive arm about Olivia's shoulders and pulling her close. 'But it's only a matter of time. I've asked Liv to marry me and she's said yes.'

'Well, congratulations!' Once again, it was Patrick Armstrong who made the first move. 'It's long overdue, if you ask me. There should never have been a divorce.'

'I agree.' Joel bent and bestowed a warm kiss on the top of Olivia's head, and no one watching them could be left in any doubt that he meant it. He looked at his mother. 'Aren't you going to give us your blessing, Mum?'

Diana's lips tightened for a moment, but then, as if the

realisation that she couldn't fight against her whole family occurred to her, she came to give them both a kiss. 'What can I say?' she exclaimed, and there was reluctant defeat in her eyes. 'I hope you'll both find the happiness you deserve.'

EPILOGUE

'CAN I go in the pool again, *please*?'

Sean dragged the word out and his father and step-mother exchanged a knowing glance.

'You've spent half the afternoon in the pool,' Olivia pointed out, deciding to play the bad cop for a change. 'Didn't your father suggest you needed a rest? If you want to come with us this evening, you need to have a sleep.'

'Well, just five minutes more,' said Sean wheedlingly. 'Then I'll go and rest for a while, I promise.' He gave Olivia a beaming smile. 'I know you don't mind, really. And after all, in a year or so you'll be wanting me to teach Natalie to swim.'

Olivia patted the baby digesting her feed on her shoulder and pulled a wry face at Joel. 'That is true,' she conceded, feeling a quiver in her insides when she met his disturbing gaze. She knew what that look meant and he was getting impatient.

'OK,' Joel said abruptly. 'Five minutes, and then you go to your room. And I don't want to hear you playing that electronic game when you're supposed to be resting. Or you'll be keeping Marsha company tonight.'

'OK, Dad.'

Sean grinned at both his parents and then dived smoothly into the water. Since coming to the United States, his swimming skills had improved tremendously. But then, having a private pool in their garden was such an advantage. Something they would seriously have to consider when they got back home.

It was just over a year since Olivia and Joel had married again, and so much had happened in those twelve short months.

Their wedding had been a quiet affair, with just their families present. Olivia had worn an oyster silk dress, which swirled about her knees, and carried a bouquet of roses and white baby's breath, that had proved to be quite prophetic in the circumstances.

Sean had acted as both pageboy and best man, his own delight enhanced by the new arrangements that had been made for his care. His mother and father had agreed to share custody from now on, Louise admitting she'd be grateful for a little time to get used to having their new baby.

Meanwhile, Olivia had found part-time employment with an estate agency in Chevingham. It meant she didn't have so far to travel and she could easily collect Sean in the afternoons when he was living with them. It worked really well, satisfying both her need to do something useful and her desire for motherhood.

The fact that Sean got on so well with his stepmother was an added bonus. And Joel, who'd been accustomed to working late into the evenings when he was living alone, found himself leaving the university as early as possible, eager to spend time with his new wife and family.

Then, towards the end of the summer, Joel had been offered a year's sabbatical in the United States. He'd be attached to a prestigious American university, and it would enable him to study their technology as well as giving him the opportunity to lecture to a different student faculty.

It had been a wonderful offer, and Olivia hadn't hesitated before encouraging him to take it. His wife and family were expected to accompany him, of course, and a house in a small town just outside Boston had been put at their disposal for the duration of their stay.

Naturally, Sean had wanted to go with them, but Joel had explained that it wouldn't be fair to his mother to take him away for so long. However, a compromise had been reached: Sean had joined them at Easter, flying the Atlantic on his own, to the envy of all his friends.

Olivia's own news had had to wait until they were settled in Massachusetts. The revelation that she was expecting a baby had filled them both with excitement and apprehension. But, in the event, their fears were groundless. Olivia had had a perfectly normal pregnancy. Their baby daughter, whom they'd called Natalie, had been born in the hospital in North Plains, instantly gaining the love and attention of both her parents and her brother.

Their year in the United States would be over in October, and, although Olivia would be sorry to leave, she was looking forward to going home. They had still to show off baby Natalie to both her grandparents and her aunt and uncle, and, despite Sean's dismay at leaving the swimming pool and the friends he'd made at his school in North Plains, he was full of excitement at the thought of telling all his English friends of the experiences he'd had and the places he'd seen.

His swim over, Sean went to take his shower and to have a nap, and Joel lifted Natalie out of his wife's arms and cradled the little girl against his chest. Natalie was three months old and thriving, and Joel had just watched Olivia feeding her, an experience he found both distracting and stimulating.

The baby reached for the finger he held in front of her, gripping it with amazing strength for her age. 'You must be tired,' he said, touching her soft cheek with amazing gentleness. 'Your mother's fed you and changed you, and you should be ready to give us a few minutes' peace.'

'Babies are unpredictable,' said Olivia, with the knowledge gained from mixing with other mothers at the baby clinic. Her eyes twinkled. 'Perhaps you ought to be honest with her and tell her you want to take her mother to bed.'

'Is it that obvious?' Joel grinned, his teeth very white against the tan that had deepened all summer long. It was much hotter in Massachusetts than it was in the north-east of England. Olivia thought he looked well-nigh irresistible in a black vest and cargo shorts, and she couldn't wait until they were alone together either.

Half an hour later, Joel rolled onto his back beside her, giving a groan of satisfaction that Olivia shared. 'I wish we weren't going out tonight,' he said regretfully. 'I'd rather stay here with you. Alone.'

Olivia looped one hand behind her head. Her hair was damp from the humidity in the atmosphere and she had no idea how tempting she looked to her husband at that moment. 'We have to go,' she said. 'Or you do, anyway. They're giving the dinner in your honour. A kind of send-off to say they'll be sorry to see you leave.'

Joel turned onto his side to face her, his fingers stroking one swollen nipple into an instantaneous peak. 'I know,' he said, his voice thickening as he bent to suckle from her breast. 'I guess I'm just feeling possessive, that's all. When we go home, I'm going to have to share you with your family again.'

Olivia tried to steel herself against what he was doing. 'I'm looking forward to seeing Dad,' she said a little breathlessly. 'According to Linda, he gets about in his new wheelchair a lot. He's even talking about getting a car with hand controls only. It's wonderful that he's feeling so much better about himself.'

'Thanks to you,' said Joel, his fingers straying down over her ribcage to her navel. His hand dipped between her legs and Olivia felt the sympathetic flood of heat his tongue and lips had engendered. 'Your coming home was the best thing that happened to all of us. Me, particularly. I can't imagine what my life was like before you came.'

'Well, I suppose I have Linda to thank for that,' she murmured weakly. And then, trying to be sensible, 'I must remember to leave a bottle of milk for Marsha to give Natalie if she wakes up while we're gone.'

Marsha had proved to be a godsend. An elderly black woman, she'd answered their ad for a housekeeper when they first arrived. Olivia had been grateful to her for so many things, not least being there when she'd gone into labour. It was Marsha who'd driven her to the hospital and made sure Joel was there when their baby was born.

'Marsha's had half a dozen children of her own. I think you can rely on her to know what to do in all circumstances,' said Joel drily. His mouth sought hers and Olivia gave up the fight to keep her head.

With a little moan, she turned onto her side and wrapped one leg over his hips, bringing his semi-aroused sex close to her throbbing core. 'OK,' she said, 'I'll stop talking. But you're wasting time now. We've only got about twenty minutes before Sean will start wondering where we are…'

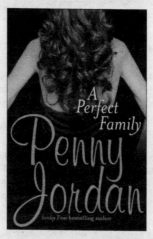

FREE

4 BOOKS AND A SURPRISE GIFT!

We would like to take this opportunity to thank you for reading this Mills & Boon® book by offering you the chance to take FOUR more specially selected titles from the Modern Romance™ series absolutely FREE! We're also making this offer to introduce you to the benefits of the Mills & Boon® Reader Service™—

- ★ **FREE home delivery**
- ★ **FREE gifts and competitions**
- ★ **FREE monthly Newsletter**
- ★ **Books available before they're in the shops**
- ★ **Exclusive Reader Service offers**

Accepting these FREE books and gift places you under no obligation to buy; you may cancel at any time, even after receiving your free shipment. Simply complete your details below and return the entire page to the address below. You don't even need a stamp!

YES! Please send me 4 free Modern Romance books and a surprise gift. I understand that unless you hear from me, I will receive 6 superb new titles every month for just £2.89 each, postage and packing free. I am under no obligation to purchase any books and may cancel my subscription at any time. The free books and gift will be mine to keep in any case.

P7ZEE

Ms/Mrs/Miss/Mr...Initials ....
BLOCK CAPITALS PLEASE

Surname ....

Address ....

....

....Postcode ....

Send this whole page to:

The Reader Service, FREEPOST CN81, Croydon, CR9 3WZ

PENGUIN BOOKS

Flying Colours

In 1793, at the tender age of just seventeen, Horatio Hornblower was forced to find his sea legs as a midshipman. After suffering his first bout of seasickness, the hapless doctor's son quickly rose through the ranks to become Admiral of the Fleet Lord Hornblower. In between, Hornblower must sail back and forth along the coasts of Europe and the Americas, repeatedly engaging or eluding the mighty ships of Napoleon and Spain. His heroic exploits in the French revolutionary war and his many other adventures in service of his country have made the name Horatio Hornblower into legend.

C. S. Forester was born in Cairo in 1899, where his father was stationed as a government official. He studied medicine at Guy's Hospital, and after leaving Guy's without a degree he turned to writing as a career. His first success was *Payment Deferred*, a novel written at the age of twenty-four and later dramatized and filmed with Charles Laughton in the leading role. In 1932 Forester was offered a Hollywood contract, and from then until 1939 he spent thirteen weeks of every year in America. On the outbreak of war he entered the Ministry of Information and later he sailed with the Royal Navy to collect material for *The Ship*. He then made a voyage to the Bering Sea to gather material for a similar book on the United States Navy, and it was during this trip that he was stricken with arteriosclerosis, a disease which l and in the Horr in twentieth-ce

Bernard Corn series of novel

left him crippled. However, he continued to write
... Hornblower novels created the great renowned sailor
... nautical fiction. He died in 1966.

... well is the bestselling author of the Sharpe